Picture Perfect

Nikki Rittenberry

For Jillian, Ashley, and Amy:
My biggest cheerleaders

Thank you for your unconditional friendship and unyielding support. And most of all, thank you for accepting my many imperfections.

"The thing that is really hard, and really amazing, is giving up on being perfect and beginning the work of becoming yourself."

—Anna Quindlen

Picture Perfect

PROLOGUE

"And this is going to be your room", Ty said as he opened the door.

Olivia glanced around the room for a moment and then slowly walked to the full-size bed positioned in front of the window. She placed her duffel bag on the worn Dukes of Hazard comforter from Ty's childhood and gradually unzipped it, revealing her most prized possessions.

"The moving truck should be here in a couple days and then we can redecorate this room with all of your stuff." Ty watched as his little sister carefully unpacked her collection of Beanie Babies, lining them along the edge of the bed against the wall, organizing them in a specific pattern that only she could decipher.

"You're really going to love it here; we're only five blocks from the beach. The water's finally warming up, too. By this time next month the temperature should reach into the upper seventies..."

The duffel bag had become deflated now that the Beanie Babies were freed. Olivia reached into the nylon material and retrieved a framed portrait of her parents. She gazed at the picture for a few long beats and then gently placed the frame on the adjacent oak nightstand.

That simple gesture tore his heart into a million little pieces. No child should have to endure the kind of grief that his little sister had. It'd been almost three weeks since he'd received the dreaded call that both his parents had been killed in a horrific car accident after leaving a restaurant in downtown Atlanta. He'd driven six torturous hours after that call to be by his little sister's side, all the while trying to imagine how a nine year old little girl would cope with such a devastating loss.

He'd arrived with the expectation that he'd have to comfort a hysterical and emotionally unstable little girl; instead he encountered a child who seemed devoid of emotions almost entirely. At the funeral it was *she* who'd consoled loved ones and friends of the family. In fact—as far as he knew—she hadn't shed a single tear. The social worker assigned to their case had assured him that *"everyone grieves differently"*, and her method—as strange as it seemed—was actually quite common.

It was important to him that Olivia was loved and nurtured. Fearing that she would be thrown into the system, raised by strangers, he'd submitted paperwork to become her legal guardian. It wasn't exactly the scenario he'd pictured for himself; he'd graduated from the fire academy last fall and had moved to Butler Island, Florida five months ago after he'd been hired by their small fire department. He didn't make a lot of money, but he had great benefits, a roof over his head, and an overwhelming sense of responsibility for his new circumstances.

"You don't have a thing to worry about. I'm going to do everything in my power to keep you with me and I promise I'll never leave you..."

Olivia looked up at her older brother and nodded, and then recited a silent prayer that the courts would grant him permanent guardianship. He was all she had and the sudden awareness terrified her. She knew he'd be giving up the one thing that most nineteen year olds' long for: independence. He was risking the best years of his life to take care of her and she didn't take that lightly. She'd decided she was going to walk the straight and narrow, refusing to give Ty a reason to regret his selfless decision to take care of her.

"Are you hungry?" she asked in her adorable southern accent. "I can make us a bowl of grits—it's my specialty."

Ty chuckled softly under his breath. Her world had been turned upside down and yet she was at it again: attempting to comfort him when it was *she* that clearly needed comforting. Their parents were dead. Gone forever. But he and Olivia were still very much alive. Somehow, he needed to guide her through this unimaginable time in her life and attempt to restore some sense of normalcy. So if making her specialty grits accomplished that—who was he to argue?

"A big bowl of grits sounds great..."

CHAPTER 1

Olivia Everitt glanced at the interstate sign.

"Thirty more miles", she mumbled softly under her breath. She'd left her apartment in New Orleans just before rush hour and had pointed her black Mini Cooper east on I-10 toward the Florida Panhandle. It'd been nine long years since she'd been home. She'd left Butler Island two days after she'd graduated high school and never looked back. Her good grades had landed her a full scholarship at a small college in Northern Louisiana where she'd studied her passion: photography.

The freedom to pack-up and leave at a moment's notice was one of the things she loved most about being a freelance photographer. She answered to no one and only pursued the projects that piqued her interests. Her first big break came three years ago after a devastating cluster of tornadoes demolished a small town just outside of Little Rock, Arkansas in early '08. She'd captured a photograph of a little girl with her back turned, standing on a mound of rumble, clutching her filthy baby doll against her side. The black and white photograph had made the cover of Adversity Magazine, well-known for documenting disasters, both natural and man-made. Since then she'd traveled the country, following catastrophe where ever it reared its ugly head.

Olivia down-shifted and steered her car away from the interstate, merging onto the desolate two-lane road that led to the slow-paced life of Butler Island. The winding road carved a path through the colossal pine forest, her surroundings seemingly unchanged since the last time she'd traveled it. This was the segment of Florida that most of the country was unaware of: far from the vain atmosphere of South Beach, hundreds of miles from the tourist traps of Orlando, and secluded from the nightlife of Panama City Beach. Traveling this road gave visitors a glimpse into how the area must have looked to settlers centuries ago: unmarred, serene, divine.

The decision to return home had been a spur-of-the-moment one. During her weekly Wednesday night conversation with Ty the night before, she'd discovered that his estranged wife, Cameron, had served him with divorce papers. It was no surprise to Olivia, but she couldn't exactly say the same about her brother.

Cameron was what the town called a "part-time local." Her family visited every year at the beginning of the summer and returned to their real home in Illinois by summers' end. Six years ago Cameron had been in town for a family reunion and had managed to get the heel of her stiletto wedged between two boards while walking on the pier. She'd stumbled and twisted her ankle just as Ty was leaving the local saloon. Always a perfect gentleman, Ty dislodged her designer shoe and assisted her to her feet. They'd spent the next few weeks together and had made a surprisingly spontaneous decision to marry.

The news of his marriage had come as a shock to Olivia—their brief courtship incapable of predicting their compatibility. He'd overextended himself to make Cameron happy: remodeling their home, installing a pool, purchasing a flashy sports car. In the end his efforts weren't enough. Several months ago she'd been having coffee with a friend at the local café when she'd spotted a good-looking executive in town for the annual Oyster Festival. The celebration was the island's only claim to fame, attracting locals and tourists from out of state. She'd had an affair with the visiting businessman and three days later, packed her bags and headed north, leaving behind a farewell letter and her two karat diamond ring.

Olivia knew that he'd been secretly holding out hope that Cameron would return home, however the sudden arrival of the divorce documents painfully signaled to Ty the finality of their separation. His world was unraveling. Although he would never outwardly admit it, he needed his little sister. He'd made a selfless decision to take care of her eighteen years ago and now it was time for her to return the favor.

"Welcome home", she mumbled as she crossed the Mainland Bridge that led to Butler Island. The town was dark and eerily quiet. She thought about what she'd be doing if she was back in New Orleans:

at ten-thirty at night, the Crescent City would just be coming to life. Butler Island took pride in its slow-paced lifestyle: the annual Oyster Festival and Winter Fest were traditionally the biggest news stories of the year. Not so great for a photographer who specialized in capturing tragedy and devastation, but Ty had nonchalantly mentioned there'd been a slew of fires the previous month and a half that had been ruled *suspicious*. It wasn't national breaking news exactly, but in her island hometown that was probably as good as it would get.

The vehicle rolled to a stop underneath the covered carport and after taking a deep breath, Olivia emerged from behind the wheel and grabbed her luggage. Once the front door was opened she stepped inside and slid her fingers up the wall in search of the light switch. Flipping the switch upward she let out a gasp... This was the home she'd grown-up in since the age of nine and she didn't recognize this place one iota.

"Sweet baby Jesus", she muttered as she glanced around the redecorated living room. Their old denim-covered couch had been replaced with a sleek, red leather sectional and the white coffee table she'd spent countless hours coloring on as a kid had been replaced with a hefty, glass-top table.

The kitchen was utterly unrecognizable as well: the outdated oak cabinetry was now painted a deep shade of gray, contrasting vividly against the white marble countertop. Appliances were stainless steel and the floor was comprised of slate. The sliding glass door had been replaced by French doors, which led to a covered patio and a rectangular-shaped pool.

Olivia retraced her steps back into the living

room and picked up her luggage before making the journey down the hall to her bedroom. She flipped the switch and stood in awe. Everything was... *exactly how she'd left it nine years ago.*

She smiled in spite of herself. The entire house had received a facelift and yet Ty had purposely left this room untouched. That had most likely infuriated Cameron, but proved to her that Ty was still hopeful that one day his sister would return.

The pink satin comforter was strewn over the antique canopy bed along with a handful of Beanie Babies she'd kept from her childhood. A swell of emotion erupted from the pit of her stomach and she blinked back the moisture as it attempted to escape her eyes. Having been gone for so many years she was uncertain how it would feel to be back. And as she collapsed onto the mattress in front of her she admitted it felt good. *Oh so good!*

Ty steered his truck onto the deserted two-lane road, the island's only fire station in his rearview mirror. He'd spent every third night here for the past eighteen years; most of those nights had been peaceful. Unfortunately that was no longer the case.

Four fires—in six weeks... that was no coincidence.

Last night's fire completely engulfed the abandoned, wood-frame home on Whippoorwill Lane. So far, the arsonist had only torched forsaken structures—and yes, they were most certainly dealing with an arsonist—but what would happen when the pyromaniac ran out of deserted properties to torch?

Lives would be in danger.

After returning to the station early this morning, he'd been greeted by the Mayor.

"If anyone asks, this fire is *'suspicious'*—nothing more, nothing less. Are we clear?" he'd said. "The last thing we need to do is unnecessarily alarm the town's residents."

Ty wondered how much longer this charade would last. Sure, Butler Island was a small town with a population of roughly a thousand residents, but they weren't ignorant. They were honest folks and they deserved to know the truth: there was a criminal among them. But that wasn't his call to make—it was Mayor Cliffburg's. So until Ty was told differently, he'd repeat the rehearsed explanation and pray the fire-starter was apprehended before a real tragedy occurred.

His commute from the station to his home on Gulf Court had only taken roughly three minutes, and as he pulled into the driveway, he wondered if maybe the physical and mental exhaustion from last night's fire was finally taking its toll: a black Mini Cooper was parked underneath the carport. No one on the small island drove that particular make and model, which could only mean one thing: his little sister had finally come home.

"Olivia... Olivia!" Ty shouted as he charged through the front door. The fatigue he'd felt moments before subsided, replaced by an overwhelming surge of anticipation. The revelation of her presence had restored his energy like a liberal dose of caffeine. He'd practically leapt from his truck upon making the discovery and surged through the front door in search of her.

"*Surprise*", she announced as she emerged

from the hallway. They rushed toward one another and embraced for almost a minute before pulling away, the silence oddly comforting.

"I can't believe you're really here!" he finally declared. "You know, you could have told me you were coming."

"What and ruin this reception?—not a chance!"

"When did you get in?"

"Late last night. I thought maybe I had the wrong house", she said as she glanced around the room. "Everything looks so..."

"Different", he offered.

"Well, yeah, but I was going to say *urban chic.*"

Ty chuckled under his breath. "Okaaay, whatever *that* means... So, how long are you here for?"

Olivia shrugged her shoulders. "For a good while, I guess."

"Good, I'm glad to hear that."

After receiving a guided tour of the recently renovated house, she made another surprising discovery: the concrete storage building in the back-yard that'd been converted into a darkroom in high school had been left untouched as well. She was moved by his unwillingness to alter her existence from this house and felt a sudden twinge of guilt for waiting as long as she had to return.

The darkroom discovery prompted Olivia to do something she hadn't done in a while: photograph something other than devastation. She'd driven five blocks and parked her Mini Cooper in the public lot before removing her shoes and reaching for her camera. The air was saturated with salt and as she descended down the wood steps, she inhaled the nostalgic aroma. The warm gulf breeze collided against her body as her toes sunk into the powdery sand and without hesitation, she raised her camera to her face and began snapping pictures of the horizon as she blindly walked forward.

She'd been walking for less than a minute before the first small wave reached her toes and a sudden fiery sensation swept across the top of her foot. Olivia tore the camera from her face and looked down as the plump, translucent jellyfish was helplessly carried away by the receding wave. She stumbled and fell to her knees in pain, almost dropping her expensive camera in the process. One quick look around only further heightened the hysteria—the entire beach was littered with jellyfish. She'd been so distracted by the beautiful scenery that she hadn't noticed the slimy sea creatures until now. In fact, it was a miracle she hadn't stepped on one before she'd reached the water.

The pain was becoming more intense with every passing moment, her skin searing from the fiery sting. She cried out in agony just as two strong arms hoisted her to her feet from behind.

"You Ok?"

"Oh, I'm just hunkey dorey!—*you?*" she asked as the large hands gripped her waist and spun her around. She came face to face with her rescuer... all six-foot, broad-shouldered inch of him.

Grant looked down at the beautiful, blonde stranger he held in his arms and smiled. The thick southern twang in her voice assuring him she wasn't from around here. "That's a pretty nasty sting you have there."

"Yeah—since when did this beach get invaded with those slimy lil' suckers?"

He chuckled under his breath. *Slimy lil' suckers?* "The tropical storm brought them in."

"But it didn't even make landfall", she reiterated.

"It didn't have to. The winds stir up the current and wash them ashore."

"Oh."

"Listen", he said as he gestured toward her foot, "we need to get you fixed up before all the toxins are released—"

"—Jesus, Joseph, and Mary—you're not gonna pee on my foot are you? Because if that's what you're plannin', then I'm gonna have to object. I'm not that kind of girl."

Grant felt the corners of his mouth turn up in a wide grin. She became more adorable and more beautiful every time she spoke. "No—I'm not going to pee on you." He pointed to the raised beach house behind her. "That's my house over there. I can have you fixed up in no time."

Olivia glanced over her shoulder at the beach house and then back at the handsome tattooed-man still holding on to her waist. "I can't do that."

"Why not?" he asked.

"Because... you're a *stranger.* How do I know you're not an ax murderer luring me to your house so you can chop me up into a bunch of little pieces?"

That did it. He couldn't contain his laughter any longer and when he met her gaze again, he realized she wasn't laughing.

"You're serious...? Honey, this is Butler Island. People leave their doors unlocked, the fruit stand on

First Street is on the honor system, and the biggest crime in the town's history was committed by a teenage girl that took a stolen jet ski on a joy ride years ago."

The beautiful woman smiled and relaxed a bit in his arms, no longer as tense as she was moments before. He removed one of his hands from her waist and offered it to her. "My name's Grant Womack and I'm a firefighter—not an ax murderer. I've got a first aid kit at the house. We can sit outside on the deck if that would make you feel more comfortable."

She looked down at his outstretched hand and bit her bottom lip before shaking it. "You can call me Olivia—not honey—and sitting on the deck would be greatly appreciated."

Grant guided her around the hundreds of jelly-fish scattered along the beach and when they reached the deck, she sat with her legs stretched out in front of her on an oversized lounge chair. He disappeared for a moment inside and then re-emerged seconds later with a bottle of distilled vinegar and a mound of gauze. He knelt down in front of her and then poured the pungent liquid over her foot.

"Ouch! Are you sure you know what you're doin'?"

"Count to ten and I promise it'll get better. The vinegar only hurts for a few seconds and then it'll begin neutralizing all the toxins the stinger re-leased... Better?"

Olivia took a deep breath and exhaled slowly though her mouth. "Yeah, a little." She studied him for a moment, which given his good looks wasn't a hardship what-so-ever. "So, the peeing thing is—"

"A myth. You're better off rinsing the sting in

the ocean than you are peeing on it." He watched as she nodded her head, retaining the information just in case she needed it for future use. "I haven't seen you around here before. Are you new in town?"

"Not exactly."

"*Not exactly...* Do you mind elaborating a little bit on that one?"

"Yes, actually, I *do* mind", she answered playfully.

Grant let out a soft chuckle and shook his head. She was a witty little thing and he liked it—he liked her. The women he'd dated on the island—if you could even call it dating—were quick to throw themselves at his feet. They were eager for a few beers and a roll in the hay, but truthfully he'd grown tired of it. It'd been a long time since he'd been intrigued by a member of the female species and the woman sitting in front of him certainly sparked his curiosity. "So, do you have any plans tonight? There's a poker tournament at my buddy's house. Some of the guys bring their wives and girlfriends..."

"Are you asking me on a date?"

"That depends, are you interested?"

"Actually, I already have plans tonight with the man in my life ", she explained.

Ouch! Grant lowered his head for a moment before meeting her green-eyed gaze again. "Well, he's a lucky man."

"Yes, he is", she said smiling. "I'll make sure to pass your message along to him." Olivia swung her legs over the side of the lounge chair and stood up.

"Do you need a ride?" he offered.

"No thanks, my car's right over there in the parkin' lot", she assured him as she gestured toward her car. "And by the way... thank you."

She started down the wood steps that led to the beach from his expansive deck. "Maybe I'll see you around", he called out as he watched her move toward the sandy shore.

"It's a small island—I'm sure you will."

CHAPTER 2

Poker night was a once a month tradition, hosted by Grant's lieutenant, and best friend, Ty. It was an opportunity to bond with his fellow "brothers" at the fire department and it was an excuse to drink a boat-load of beer, too. He arrived at Ty's house a few minutes late, the boys steadily hassling him over the game delay. The guys were already seated at the large dining room table as he walked to the fridge to snag an ice cold beer. He glanced through the window pane and saw the women huddled around the patio table—exchanging gossip no doubt. Not wanting to disturb their whispering campaign and cause further delay from the tournament, he gave a quick wave and then joined the guys at the dining room table.

"Glad you could make it", Ty announced dryly.

"Oh, I wouldn't miss taking your money for the world, bro."

Ty began shuffling the cards and then swiftly distributed five cards a piece to his self, as well as the seven guys sitting at the table. After everyone had an opportunity to take a look at their dealt hands, Eddie Yates placed the first bet, tossing his poker chips into the middle of the table. "I have to tell you, Ty: that was one hell of a surprise", he said.

"Yeah, did you know she was coming?" Jimmy Phillips asked.

"Nope—I was just as surprised as the rest of you."

"What the hell are you guys talking about?" Grant interjected.

"My sister's in town." Ty placed his cards face down on the table and then stood from his chair. He walked to the French doors and asked his sister to come inside whenever she had a moment and then sat back down at the table.

Grant was busy studying his cards, oblivious to the silhouette walking toward him—that is until the silhouette opened her mouth to speak.

"Alright boys, this had better be good—I'm not playin' waitress tonight!"

Grant immediately looked up from his cards. That adorable southern accent had been distracting him all fucking day.

"Grant, I'd like you to meet my baby sister, Olivia."

Olivia reached her hand toward Grant. "It's a pleasure to meet you... Grant, right?" she asked smiling.

Grant chuckled softly under his breath. Earlier in the day he'd had his hands on her waist when he'd rescued her on the beach. And on those incredibly sexy legs when he'd knelt in front of her while applying first aid to her foot. "Yeah... Same goes."

She removed her hand from his and took a step back. "Alright, now that I've managed to meet all the new faces at this table—you can proceed with your silly lil' *Go Fish* game!" She gave Grant a wink and then turned and walked away.

"It's not *Go Fish*—it's poker!" Ty shouted over his shoulder.

"Same difference", she countered before joining the women back on the patio.

Olivia closed the French doors behind her and walked toward her seat.

"So, it looks as though you just met Butler Island's most eligible bachelor", Lana Phillips announced.

Olivia took her seat and glanced around the table at six pairs of eyes staring back at her. "Did I miss something? Why is everyone staring at me like that?"

"Oh c'mon, Olivia—did you see the way Grant just looked at you?—like you were the prime rib at an all-you-can-eat buffet?" Jenny Carson asked.

Olivia tucked her honey-blonde hair behind one of her ears. "Alright, look—please don't take this the wrong way, but you ladies need to get out more. And by *'out more'*, I mean something far more excitin' than poker night and preferably off of Butler Island."

The group of women got a good laugh out of that. Most of the locals had never even left the state of Florida, let alone the county. They had no idea about what life was like beyond the Mainland Bridge. Olivia did, though. She'd traveled all over the continental United States for her career. She'd witnessed real life firsthand; experienced it with open arms and had the scars, both physical and emotional, to prove it.

"I'd give anything for *that* man to look at me like that", Tonya Woods mumbled.

"Oh, please—*you're married!*" announced Jenny. "Does Mark know about your secret crush?"

"Are you kidding me?—like I would just come right out and say it: 'Here's your dinner, honey. How's your meatloaf? And by the way, did you know that my mouth drops open like an idiot whenever Grant walks into the room?'"

Laughter erupted from around the patio table and when they finally settled down, Olivia's curiosity finally got the best of her. "So, tell me about him. What's his story?"

"Well, he's been at the fire department for about five years—"

"And let's not leave out the most important part", Jenny interjected. "He's great at friendship, but he's a lousy boyfriend."

"What do you mean?" asked Olivia

"She means he's a die-hard womanizer—a serial dater. *A player.* I heard from Jimmy that Grant's never had a serious relationship before and judging by his previous dating record, he probably never will", Lana shared.

"Hmm, that's very interesting..." *Very interesting indeed.* Olivia had never had a serious relationship either. Oh, she'd certainly come close a time or two, but every time her previous boyfriends' began dropping subtle hints that they were interested in something more serious, she'd panicked. She was completely aware that her fear of love and commitment set her apart from the other ninety-nine percent of the female population, but she did have her reasons.

Losing her parents at such a young age had deeply affected her. She'd never felt so grief-stricken and vulnerable in her entire life, before or since that dreadful night. Aside from her brother, Ty, she kept all relationships with the male species at arm's length. Her biggest phobia—other than heights—was to revisit the kind of pain she'd endured then. To allow her heart to become accessible, leaving her weak and defenseless. She liked to have complete and utter control of her life; just thinking about losing it made her panic.

But she had to admit, she was incredibly intrigued by Grant. Looking at him was certainly no hardship. His light brown hair dared her to run her fingers through it; his eyes were ice-blue, but there was nothing cold about them. His long lashes were borderline envious. And those lips...

Okay, she was admittedly curious—even more so by his playboy reputation. He wasn't looking for anything serious and neither was she. She only planned on being in town for a few months and spending time with a drop-dead-gorgeous fireman would give her a sense of adventure in this slow-paced island town.

Grant glanced at the shrinking stack of poker chips in front of him and then at his cards. *Damn it!* There was no doubt about it: he'd been dealt a very shitty hand this round.

"So, what brings your sister to town?" he asked, hoping the conversation was enough to distract Ty from winning yet another round.

"Hell if I know—Olivia is... spontaneous and adventurous by nature."

"Spontaneous and adventurous...?"

"Yep, I raised her from the age of nine and two days after she graduated, she up and left and hasn't been back until now. Her being gone is partly my fault, though."

"Why's that?" Grant asked curiously.

"Well, let's just say Olivia didn't hide the fact that she wasn't a big fan of Cameron and Cameron felt the same way about her. I traveled to New Orleans a couple times to visit, but she'd always declined to come back home."

"Ah." He was beginning to like her more by the minute. He wasn't a big fan of Cameron either. In fact, he was probably the only one on the entire island that saw through her innocent guise.

Grant placed twenty dollars worth of chips in the center of the table; the only chance he had to win this game was to rely heavily on distracting and bluffing his opponents. "Any idea how long she's staying?"

Ty met his twenty dollar bet and raised him fifteen. "I have no idea. She didn't give me a departure date. But knowing her, she won't be able to stay idle for long..."

After Grant reluctantly removed himself from the tournament, he grabbed another beer and headed outside for a breath of fresh air. He ambled toward the pool where Olivia was sitting with her pants' legs rolled up to her knees; her legs swishing softly in the chilly water. He settled down beside her, removing his flip flops and rolling his jeans, submerging his feet into the cool water as well. "So, the man in your life you spoke about earlier was...?"

"My brother, Ty", she said smiling.

"And you didn't feel the need to tell me that the 'man in your life' was also a fireman because...?"

"Because you didn't ask", she responded playfully.

Grant chuckled under his breath and then gestured toward her injury. "How's the foot doing?"

Olivia straightened her leg, lifting her foot out of the water. "Well, it's a lil' tender, but I'm a tough girl."

"I don't doubt that for a minute", he said as he flashed a heated smile.

Oh, yeah. Spending time with the island's most eligible bachelor was going to be fun. "I take it since you're out here flirtin' with me and the rest of the guys are still inside, playing cards, means you didn't do so well tonight."

She's good—real good. "Flirting? Is that what I was doing?" he asked, grinning.

"Uh-huh. That's precisely what you were doin'."

Grant put his hands up in surrender. "Ok... guilty! And to answer your first question, the game didn't go very well for me tonight. I was sort of *distracted*."

"Oh yeah? Why's that?" she asked curiously as she took a sip of red wine.

"Because... I was too busy staring at you."

Spoken like a true player, she thought. This was going to be fun. He was probably used to women falling at his feet, melting into a willing puddle of lust at the sight of his sinfully suggestive smile, but he hadn't had the pleasure of crossing paths with her yet. Make no mistake, her extremities felt like a heaping mound of overcooked noodles every time he looked at her with those eager, ice-blue eyes—the same blue eyes sweeping across her mouth right now—but he certainly didn't need to know that. Guys like Grant enjoyed *"the chase"* and judging by the reactions from some of the women earlier, he hadn't engaged in a challenging pursuit of the opposite sex in quite some time.

"Aw, I'm flattered—you're worried about me. *That's really sweet.*"

Sweet? He'd been called a lot of things in his thirty-three years, but *"sweet"* wasn't one of them. Grant laughed in spite of himself. For some strange reason, she had that effect on him. "So, are you going to be around for Ty's annual Halloween party next weekend?"

"Are you kiddin' me?—of course! I love Halloween."

"Yeah? What's your costume?" he asked.

Olivia leaned her weight back on her hands. "Hmm, I don't know yet. Any suggestions?"

"Oh, I don't know... nudist colony member?" he suggested as he winked at her.

She felt her bones beginning to melt into that willing puddle of lust she thought about moments earlier. It was a good thing her feet were submerged in the chilly water; if the conversation continued much longer she might be forced to submerge her entire body. He was slick, but she wasn't going to give him the satisfaction of showing him what he was doing to her insides right now.

"Hmm, I'll have to keep that one in mind..."

CHAPTER 3

Butler Island contained all of the essentials the small town needed: a modest-sized police and fire department, a post office, a humble grocery store and neighborhood pharmacy. The majority of the businesses on the island were located along the boardwalk. There was an antique shop, a delicious bakery and café, restaurants, a saloon, and several little stores that sold everything from clothes to seashells to fishing poles.

Olivia awoke the next morning with a clear goal in mind: find a Halloween costume. She figured she would travel to the boardwalk and check out the Seasonal Bazaar, a small boutique that specialized in inventory to suit every season and holiday of the year. She loosely braided her long blonde hair and slipped into an old pair of comfortable jeans and a white tank top when the doorbell rang.

"Coming!" she called out as she approached the door.

"Oh my goodness, it really is true... You're

here!" Kendall Porter cried.

"In the flesh! How are you?" Olivia asked as she stepped forward to give Kendall a hug. Kendall was Olivia's childhood best friend. They'd stayed in touch throughout the years, although not as often as she would have liked. Kendall had left Butler Island for college as well, but had returned after graduation to manage the small neighborhood pharmacy on the island.

"Every thing's been great."

She still looked the same: Tall, black shoulder-length hair, large amber eyes and an envious olive complexion. She was a beauty, both inside and out.

"How did you know I was here?" Olivia asked.

Kendall gave her a look of disbelief. "You have been gone a long time... This is Butler Island, remember? Word travels fast here!"

"Yeah, guess I'd better get used to that again..."

Kendall accompanied Olivia to the Seasonal Bazaar, in search of a costume for herself as well. They'd been sifting through the racks for several minutes before Olivia's curiosity got the best of her. "I have a question for you."

"Ok—shoot."

"What do you know about Grant Womack?" Kendall held up a pink princess costume, asking for her opinion. When Olivia wrinkled her nose and shook her head in disapproval, Kendall returned the satin garment back to the rack.

"Well, besides being the most eligible bachelor in the county?—not much... He's a fairly private guy. He is Mr. Gibson's grandson, though."

"Really? I didn't know that... I guess that explains the beach house then."

Kendall froze and looked up at Olivia in anticipation. "You were at his beach house?— *When?*—and I want all the raunchy details, too!"

"I'm sorry to disappoint you, but it wasn't like that", she assured her. She went on to tell her about her jellyfish encounter and how Grant had been there to administer first aid. Olivia finally stumbled across a costume she liked and held it up to get Kendall's approval.

"I think that one's perfect! And do you want to know what else I think?"

"Of course."

"I have a gut feeling that you're going to become familiar with that beach house and the man who lives in it..."

Kendall and her gut feelings. Her intuition, although at times mysterious, was also very reliable. And just to make sure, Olivia had to ask. "What do you mean?"

"Oh, c'mon—he's gorgeous, he's single, and he's *totally* into you!"

"He is not—he's Ty's best friend. He's just trying to be polite. And besides... how do you know who Grant's '*into*'?"

Kendall shot Olivia a hollow look. "Need I remind you again? Gossip circulates quickly on this island."

"Oh yeah, I almost forgot..."

"Okay, I think this is the last box", Ty announced as he carefully stepped down from the ladder.

Olivia sat on the cool concrete floor of the carport with her legs tucked underneath her. She'd already opened the first box of Halloween decorations and was nostalgically sifting through them when Ty knelt down beside her.

"I can't believe you kept this all these years", she said as she clutched the homemade Halloween trivet she'd constructed in her Home Economics class in the seventh grade. It'd been fabricated from orange and black ceramic beads and Popsicle sticks. She'd been so proud of her creation then and had given it to Ty as a gift. But seeing it now through her adult eyes, she realized how pathetic it actually looked.

"Of course, I kept it."

"Ty, it's the ugliest darn trivet I've ever seen! You mean to tell me that you still put this out on the counter every year?" she asked in disbelief.

"Every year."

"That couldn't have made Cameron very happy..." She watched as he wiped his hand down the front of his face. He was hurting and she wished more than ever that she could absorb the pain he was experiencing so that he wouldn't have to endure it.

He let out a sigh and then met his little sister's gaze. "No—she wasn't fond of the trivet..."

"Or me", Olivia added. "I want you to know that me being gone all this time had nothing to do with you... It's no secret that Cameron and I didn't like each other very well, but I saw how happy she made you. And I figured your happiness was long overdue."

"Liv, I'm so very sorry."

"Sorry? For what? You have absolutely nothing to feel sorry for", she assured him.

"Yeah, I do. Cameron made you feel as though this was no longer your home—"

"That's right—*Cameron*—not you."

"Yeah, but I let her..."

Olivia wrapped her arms around her brother and gave him a squeeze. "It's okay—that's behind us now. This is a new beginning—for *both* of us."

"I'm so glad you're here", he mumbled as he hugged her back.

"Me, too", she said before pulling away. "Enough of this emotional mushy stuff—we've got some Halloween decoratin' to do..."

An unexpected cold front had arrived earlier in the day, causing temperatures on the island to plummet into the mid-fifties upon nightfall. Grant parked his truck along the street in front of Ty's house. He'd chosen to dress as a 1920's gangster this year, sporting a black and white striped suit and black fedora. He emerged from his truck with a toy Tommy-gun in hand and then headed inside.

He was greeted by a grinning Ty, decked out in a flight suit and aviator glasses; looking like "Iceman" from the movie *Top Gun*. "Well, this gives a whole new meaning to 'wing man', doesn't it?"

"Nice monkey suit, asshole", Ty responded.

Grant stepped inside and placed his beer in the refrigerator before taking inventory of all the various costumes in the room. Eddie was dressed as a pirate, complete with an eye patch and fake parrot attached to one of his shoulders. Jimmy Phillips and his wife, Lana, were dressed as a tough-looking biker and biker-babe, and Randall Burns was dressed as the blue guy from *Avatar*. He was amazed by the crowd's creativity, but there was one person in particular that impressed him most.

Olivia.

She was standing on the patio by the stainless steel, outdoor heater in a skimpy little referee costume, hair down in large, voluminous curls like a Texas beauty queen. Her snug referee ensemble clung to her mouth-watering curves, the hem falling mid-thigh, revealing the sexiest pair of legs he'd ever seen. She wore black stiletto boots that rose midway up her lower legs and a pair of black and white tube socks that settled just below her knees. Unable to resist, he opened the French doors and ambled toward her.

Olivia met his astonished gaze and smiled, throwing up her hands in front of her as though she were surrendering. "Don't shoot", she uttered as he approached.

His eyes journeyed down the length of her body and then stalled at her cleavage. "I don't know—you don't look so *innocent* right now…"

Olivia cocked her head sideways and cleared her throat, distracting his attention away from her breasts. "Watch it, Womack—you just might find yourself with a penalty."

Sexual innuendos, one of his favorite games. Grant flashed a wicked grin. "Oh yeah? Which one would that be?"

"Unsportsman-like conduct", she responded playfully. Olivia swept her gaze down Grant this time, pausing when she reached the large bulge in his pants. "I like your Tommy-gun. It's so… *big.*"

Holy shit. "Who's on the verge of a penalty now?"

Olivia took a step closer and rose onto her toes so that her mouth was inches from his ear. "I'm just the ref; I call 'em like I see 'em", she whispered before she walked away.

"She's somethin' else, isn't she?" Randall asked as he joined Grant on the patio.

Grant took a pull from his beer, eyeing Olivia until she disappeared inside. "Yeah... How well do you know her?"

"Olivia?" Randall asked. "We grew up together. She was a year younger than me, but she was still one of my closest friends. Would've given anything to be more than friends, though."

"Had a secret crush, did ya?"

Randall chuckled softly as he tucked his hands under his arms. "Me and half the town's teenage male population! But she didn't really date much back then..."

"Why not?" Grant asked as he crossed his arms over his chest, turning his attention to the electric-blue man standing beside him.

Randall shrugged his shoulders. "Partly because she was too busy causing a ruckus to be tied down in a relationship. And partly because every guy on the island knew her free-spirit couldn't be tamed..."

The party was a big success. It was late—or early the following morning—before the crowd had thinned. Kendall had been talking to Ty on the couch when he'd placed the back of his head against the sleek red leather and closed his eyes. She thought he was just resting them for a moment, but when he began to snore she realized he'd passed out. "Um, Olivia?" she called out to the kitchen.

"Yeah?"

"Ty's out cold."

"What?" Olivia moved from behind the counter and walked into the living room. Ty's glasses were crooked and his mouth was slightly parted. Olivia gave him a firm nudge, which only made him snore louder. "Poor guy—he probably hasn't had a decent night of sleep since Cameron left a couple of months ago..."

"Bitch", Kendall murmured.

"Yeah, my thoughts exactly."

Grant returned from the restroom and watched as the nurse and the referee huddled around Ty, observing him sleep. He quietly crept up behind them and when he was inches away from Olivia's ear, he came to a halt. "Am I missing something?" he asked as the girls leapt from the couch in a startled panic.

"Don't do that!" Olivia exclaimed, reaching for her chest to sooth her racing heartbeat. "You nearly scared my britches off!"

Grant raised an eyebrow. "Well, in that case—let me try again."

Kendall looked at Grant and then back at Olivia. There was so much sexual tension in the room it nearly smothered her. "Okaaay—I think this is my cue to go." She reached for her purse lying on the glass sofa table and fumbled around for her keys. "Great party, by the way."

Without tearing his eyes from the sexy referee in front of him, Grant inquired about her ability to drive and after Kendall reiterated that she was perfectly fine, she stepped out into the cool night and closed the door behind her.

"And then there were two", he said as he looked into Olivia's emerald eyes.

"Well, actually three if you count the unconscious aviator lying on the couch. You think maybe we could carry him to his bed?" she asked.

"I think we can manage."

After the gangster and referee tucked the drunken aviator into bed, they cleared the kitchen and patio of empty cups and beer bottles, essentially erasing any evidence that a party had taken place there hours earlier. The temperature felt as though it had dropped a few more degrees as Grant and Olivia sauntered back onto the patio for one last drink. They huddled around the outdoor heater, sitting on a lounge chair next to one another as though it were a bench. The pool light had a red cover fastened to it, creating an illusion of bloody water, and various fake body parts floated randomly along the surface.

"I missed this", Olivia said as she gestured toward the pool. "Ty always decorated the entire house for Halloween every year when I was growin' up. We didn't have a pool then, but he always had a lot of creativity."

"He's a good guy."

"Yeah", Olivia sighed. "He sure is…"

"He has a lot of decorations and quite an imagination, too", Grant shared as he pointed to a plastic foot floating by.

"Well, we accumulated a lot of this over the years. When I first came to live with him, the only decoration he owned was a ceramic pumpkin candy dish that mom had given him. When my parents were alive, they decorated the house from top to bottom with spooky decorations and since Halloween was my favorite time of year, Ty made sure we kept the tradition goin'."

"So, Halloween was your favorite holiday?"

"Uh-huh—still is", she offered.

Grant turned his body slightly to face her. "Why?"

Olivia shrugged her shoulders. "I don't know—I guess it's because it's the only night out of the year that you can put on a costume and transform into someone else. You can pretend, for one night, to lead a completely different life... And I have no idea why I just told you that!" She confessed as she emerged from her trance.

Olivia turned and met his intense gaze. "Don't", she demanded.

"Don't what?"

"Don't look at me like that!"

Clearly amused, Grant revealed a charming smile. "How am I looking at you?"

"Like... like you think I'm completely *crazy* or somethin'."

He couldn't take it any longer. Without hesitation, he reached behind her head and cupped the back of her neck, gently caressing her jaw with his thumb. "I wasn't thinking you were crazy... I was thinking about what it'd be like to kiss you."

"Oh", she whispered.

Grant licked his suddenly dry lips and then leaned forward. He pressed his mouth against her soft, warm lips, giving her an opportunity to pull away if she was having second thoughts.

She didn't.

Instead her lips parted, inviting him for a taste. One slick stroke of her sweet tongue and he was gone. He angled his head to deepen the kiss and heard the sweetest moan escape from the back of her throat.

Olivia clenched his light brown hair in her hands, wanting to feel closer to him—suddenly needing to be closer. Every nerve-ending was on alert, her skin hypersensitive to his gentle touch. His hands grazed down her back, sending shivers down her spine and spreading warmth across her body like a sultry New Orleans summer day.

"I should probably go", he whispered against her mouth. He didn't want to though, damn it. What he really wanted to do was strip her out of her referee ensemble and rack up a slew of *penalties*. He wanted to play dirty; he wanted to make a touchdown...

Olivia tilted her head to the side, giving him better access to the sensitive spot on her neck just below her ear. "Yeah, you should", she uttered breathlessly.

She gasped when his mouth grazed the ticklish area just below her ear. She could feel the warmth of his breath on her delicate skin and when he began spreading open-mouth kisses along her jaw, her eyes rolled back into her head.

Every moan of pleasure, every quickened breath aroused him. He felt as though he was being engulfed by lust-saturated quicksand; his body fighting to stay in control, every subtle movement threatening to consume him. He knew if he didn't regain his self-control now, the kissing would escalate. And that couldn't happen.

She was Ty's little sister—*his very beautiful, sexy, irresistible little sister.*

Game over.

Reluctantly, Grant tore his mouth away and stood up. "I'm sorry", he said before walking away. He adjusted the growing bulge in his pants and made a mental note to grab an icepack from the freezer on his way out to soothe the severe case of blue balls he was going to have by the time he drove the five blocks to his beach house.

Olivia ran the tip of her fingers over her tingling lips, still wet and swollen from his kiss. She observed him as he disappeared inside the house, leaving her alone on the lounge chair they'd shared, aroused, with a mixture of emotions. She was surprised by how easily she'd lost control.

Yeah, she really needed to watch that next time.

Next time?—Jesus, Joseph and Mary—*listen to her*. Their kiss had quickly ignited into a raging fire-storm. And then as quickly as it'd started, he pulled away. A gentleman-like gesture?—or a quick recovery over a drunken lapse in judgment? She wondered. The answer to that question: Only time would tell...

CHAPTER 4

The sweet smell of freshly baked doughnuts saturated the air inside Olivia's Mini Cooper, becoming increasingly more intense with every passing mile. Ty had been hounding her to come by the fire station to visit and even though it had been a while, she knew better than to arrive without treats.

Olivia hadn't spoken to Grant since their kiss five days ago. The kiss had been... *well, it had been amazing*. But maybe he'd regretted it. Maybe the brave-juice he'd ingested throughout the evening had altered his judgment. Maybe he'd awoke the following morning with an aching head and clarity of what he'd done.

Since the moment he'd assisted her to her feet on the beach after her jellyfish encounter, she'd wondered. Wondered what it'd be like to kiss him and now that she *knew*...

Kissing had always been rather trivial to her. Well, that's not exactly true. She'd once went on a date with a fellow freelance photographer and he'd nearly choked her with his tongue—needless to say there wasn't a second date. So maybe kissing wasn't *trivial*, but it also hadn't been pivotal either.

Until she'd kissed Grant.

Now she was beginning to think that maybe kissing wasn't just a means to an end. Perhaps it was meant to be savored. Her kiss with Grant had been perfect: aggressive, yet not overbearing—lustful, yet not sloppy. There was no doubt about it: the man could kiss—

"Damn it", she muttered as she came to a stop. She'd been obsessing over the kiss and had missed her turn. Olivia made an illegal U-turn along the abandoned two-lane road and headed back to the street she'd passed.

Take a deep breath and pull yourself together!

She steered her car down the long drive that led to the hidden fire station. Okay, no more driving with three dozen freshly baked doughnuts in the car. Clearly it affected her mind.

Yeah, blame it on the doughnuts...

After snagging the last parking spot in the small lot she removed her key from the ignition and inhaled a deep, calming breath. Ty was going to be happy that she'd finally made the time to visit the station. She hated to disappoint him and besides— she was hoping to run into Grant so that she could apologize for the other night.

Alright, pep talk's over. Time to get inside and get this visit over with.

Olivia gripped the three rectangular doughnut boxes from the passenger seat and strolled toward the open bay. It housed the island's only fire truck and a myriad of memories from her childhood and adolescence. When she was within reach, she slowly glided her fingertips along the side of the fire truck, reminiscing about the first time she'd sat inside. She was nine and Ty had given her permission to sit behind the wheel and pretend to drive. Her feet dangled from the seat, fidgeting with excitement as he turned on the siren and coaxed her to beep the horn. She closed her eyes as she recalled the vivid memory and felt the corners of her mouth turn up in a wide grin.

Grant left the claustrophobic firehouse kitchen in search of some fresh air. He hadn't been able to get Olivia, or the mind-blowing kiss they'd shared, out of his head all week. No matter how hard he tried, he couldn't escape the image of her emerald eyes staring back into his. She was like a Picasso painting: beautiful, intriguing. Rebellious.

As soon as he'd become aware that she was Ty's little sister, he'd told himself to back off. It didn't matter that he was incredibly attracted to her; she was off limits to him. She'd been rambling on about how Halloween was her favorite holiday and when he'd asked why, something unexpected happened: She softened that tough-girl exterior and exposed a hint of vulnerability.

He knew the basics about her story. Her parents died when she was young and Ty had raised her. He'd asked around about her to the people on the island—nonchalantly, of course—and everyone pretty much told him the same thing: *"She's a sassy southern belle. A free-spirited beauty. An angel with devilish spontaneity. A gorgeous doll with a tough-as-*

nails attitude." He figured she'd had to be. Anyone who lost their parents as unexpectedly and tragically as she had learned how to coat themselves with armor to prevent experiencing another loss.

The kiss was a spontaneous reaction to her vulnerableness—a comforting gesture, like patting someone on the back when they choked...

Ah, hell, who was he kidding? He liked her. He liked talking to her, hearing her laugh.

And he *really* liked kissing her.

He'd had every intention of calling her—even came close a few times—but ultimately hesitated. Ty was his best friend and he wasn't sure how he would feel about him dating his little sister. It was no secret that Ty was *overprotective* when it came to Olivia and so Grant knew he'd have to proceed with caution.

A steady stream of brisk morning air rushed across his skin as he stepped into the open bay. He briefly closed his eyes, inhaling a satisfying breath and when he opened them, the woman he'd been obsessing over was standing approximately fifty feet in front of him. He studied her for a moment: she was balancing three large white boxes in one hand; gently running her feminine fingertips along the surface of the fire truck with the other. Her eyes were closed and the corners of her mouth were slightly turned upward, suggesting she was thoroughly enjoying her nostalgic trance.

Grant ambled forward, careful to tread softly and when he reached her side, he paused briefly to take in her beauty. She'd been concentrating diligently, completely unaware that Grant was standing by her side watching her.

"You must have ESP", he uttered softly, inches

from her ear.

Olivia opened her eyes and gasped for a breath of air. Startled, she instinctively leapt back and quickly juggled the three doughnut boxes to prevent them from falling.

"Sweet baby Jesus! What are you doing here?" She shouted.

Grant reached for the tumbling doughnut boxes and steadied them with his large hands before meeting her gaze. He really hadn't meant to frighten her, but discovering her standing next to the fire truck, reveling in what appeared to be fond memories from her childhood, fascinated him. The expression on her face had been peaceful and carefree and he savored every second of it.

He smiled at her stupefied demeanor. "I work here, remember...?"

Olivia took a deep breath and sighed as she spoke. "Right. It's all coming back to me now", she answered.

Grant removed his hands from the boxes and placed them safely in his pockets. He didn't trust himself not to touch her again. "What are *you* doing here?"

Raising the boxes slightly, she gave them a slight jiggle. "I brought everyone doughnuts. Ty's been hounding me to stop by for weeks now—and *why do I have ESP?*" she asked confusedly.

"Because, I was just thinking about you and now you're here..." An awkward silence lurked between them for a moment and in an attempt to gain comfort, Grant stepped in front of her and leaned his shoulder against the fire engine. He blew out a puff of air and studied his work boots as he began. "Look,

Olivia, I've been meaning to call you and—"

"—It's okay—no need to explain. You and I both probably had too much to drink and I'm sure if we'd been sober, nothing would've happened."

Grant tore his attention away from his shoes and pinned her with his stare. "Is that what you really think? Because I've been fighting the urge to kiss you ever since I rescued you on the beach."

Her expression remained carefree, although her stiffened posture revealed a glimpse of vulnerability. "You didn't rescue me—I'm not a damsel in distress", she stated.

"Oh yeah?" Clearly amused, he crossed his arms and felt the corners of his mouth rise. "What would you call it then?"

Without missing a beat, she answered with a wide grin. "Relocation and first aid administration."

Grant felt a gut-busting laugh erupt from deep within. She was such a tough girl—never wanting to admit she'd needed his help that day. Never wanting to show any outward signs of weakness. "Well, that's certainly a first."

When he'd finally regained his composure, he pointed at her with his finger and flashed a heated smile. "You owe me a date."

Hearing him laugh warmed her soul and when he exposed that smile—*the one that could melt a woman's panties in ten seconds or less*—she couldn't help but feel a rush of adventure. She felt the tension she'd been living with for the past five days slowly recede. He'd enjoyed the kiss every bit as much as she had and he was clearly attempting to put plans in motion to kiss her again. A significant part of her wanted to jump at the opportunity to spend an evening with him on the spot. But what would be the fun in that?

That's the kind of reaction he's accustomed to.

He says "jump" and they say "how high?" It was time for Grant to sweat a little bit.

Heavens to Betsy—this was going to be fun! "You mean the drunken Halloween kiss wasn't repayment enough for your services?" she asked playfully.

"Nope—have any plans for tomorrow night?"

"As a matter of fact, I was thinkin' of color coordinatin' my closet", she attempted in her best poker face.

Grant laughed, but his expression slowly faded when he realized she wasn't smiling any longer. "You're serious?"

"Uh-huh", she responded, her lips desperately struggling to conceal her growing grin.

"You're not going to make this easy on me, are you?" he mumbled as he wiped his hand down his face.

"Are you implyin' that I'm playin' hard to get, Womack?"

Grant licked his lips and smiled. "Well, you were a referee for Halloween—you seem to enjoy games."

"Alright, what do you have in mind?"

Grant shrugged his shoulders attempting to appear at ease, but truthfully he was a mangled mess of nerves. He'd practically begged her to go on a date with him—*that was certainly a first.* He couldn't recall ever having to persuade a woman to spend time with him, but then again he'd never met anyone quite as unique and fascinating as Olivia. "I don't know... I was thinking dinner—even referees have to eat, right?"

"Alright, I'll tell you what... I'll *think* about it..."

He watched as she sauntered away from him and he couldn't help but smile. In his thirty-three years he'd never encountered a woman so indecisive, so determined to have the upper hand. He felt like a racing greyhound chasing the mechanical rabbit; no matter how diligently he followed, it was always slightly out of reach. Of course, he wasn't chasing a stuffed bunny—he was seeking quality time with a sassy southern belle. He liked that she wasn't overly eager. It was intriguing, exciting, and incredibly sexy...

Seconds after placing the boxes on the over-sized dining table, the feeding frenzy began. Olivia was suddenly surrounded by a half dozen hungry firemen. "Am I in the right place? I didn't accidently drive to the police station, did I?" she stated as she glanced around the room.

Ty put his arm around his little sister and kissed the top of her head. "Cops aren't the only ones who like doughnuts, you know. Especially when they're doughnuts from Anderson's Bakery."

Randall Burns opened the box, wearing an unmistakable expression of bliss. "Mmm, they're still warm... Thanks DD!" he shouted as he stuffed the Swiss chocolate-drizzled doughnut in his mouth.

Grant had just returned to the kitchen when he'd overheard Randall babbling. *DD?* He'd clearly been speaking to Olivia, but those weren't her initials. "Okay, what does 'DD' stand for?" he finally asked.

Jimmy Phillips tore his mouth away from his doughnut long enough to give him a very brief explanation. "Daredevil."

Grant turned his attention to Olivia and raised his brows. "Daredevil, huh?"

She met his astonished gaze and smiled as Ty placed his arm around his sister's shoulders. "Grant, you are in the presence of a living legend. It's a funny story—*although it wasn't so funny at the time*... This girl right here stole Mr. Baker's jet ski when she was fifteen and took it on a three hour joyride!"

Grant couldn't believe what he was hearing! He'd heard about the free-spirited teenage girl that'd hijacked a jet ski, but no one had ever uttered her name. He'd always thought it was an urban legend, unable to comprehend something so outrageous happening on the slow-paced island. "That was *YOU?*" he asked in disbelief.

"Well, first of all I didn't steal it—stealin' implies I had no intention of returnin' it—I *borrowed it*. And Mr. Baker should've known better than to leave that Jet Ski with the key in the ignition and a full tank of gas. And finally, I can't be held entirely responsible—it was all Randall's fault."

"*Randall?* How was it Randall's fault?" he asked incredulously.

"Because I *dared* her to do it..." Randall explained as he licked the chocolate from his fingertips.

"Alright, alright—what's all the commotion about", Chief Handler interjected as he emerged from his office. He was a large, intimidating man with a deep growling voice, but Olivia knew that outward appearances were often misleading; Chief Handler was nothing more than an oversized teddy bear.

"Good mornin', Chief", she said as she stepped away from Ty.

"Olivia...?" His roughened expression suddenly

turned softer as he opened his arms, encouraging her to experience one of his infamous bear hugs.

She rushed toward him, but was unable to wrap her arms around him completely. He'd always been a large man and in the nine years she'd been away, he'd obviously managed to expand his waist circumference by more than a few inches.

"I heard you were back in town and I was beginning to wonder if you were ever going to stop by and see me!" Chief placed his hands on her shoulders and took a step back. "Look at you—all grown up! Hell, it seems like just yesterday you were sitting in the fire truck pretending to drive!"

"Yeah, it does... I hope you're hungry; I brought three dozen doughnuts from Anderson's Bakery."

Chief smiled and then grabbed his belly, giving his blubber a slight jiggle. "Are you kidding me?—I'm always hungry!" Cupping his hand over his mouth, he continued in a hushed tone, "And if by chance you happen to run into my wife, please be sure to exclude what I'm about to do, okay?"

Olivia watched as he picked up a paper plate and eagerly piled four doughnuts on top before licking his fingertips. No wonder he didn't want Mrs. Handler to find out. He wasn't eating the *"breakfast of champions"*; he was moments away from consuming a heart attack on a plate. "Don't worry, Chief, you're secret is safe with me..."

Chief Handler devoured his first doughnut in roughly three bites and then turned to face Ty. "Everitt, I need to speak with you in my office about the state fire marshal's latest report."

"Alright Chief, I'll be right there." Ty glanced toward Olivia and gave her a smirk. "If I'm not back in thirty minutes—pull the fire alarm", he whispered wryly before he turned and walked away.

"Should we save a few doughnuts for Jarrod?" Tommy Carson asked.

"C'mon, man. You honestly think he's gonna eat one?" Jimmy questioned.

"Good point."

Olivia looked at the men surrounding the doughnuts. "Okay—who's Jarrod and why wouldn't he want any doughnuts?"

"Because, those things will kill ya..."

Olivia turned around just as a tall, lean, shirtless man emerged from the hallway. He'd obviously just completed a workout: his wet, blonde hair falling across his forehead, his chest glistening with sweat. His eyes were dark and mysterious. And they were currently gliding across her body.

"I don't believe we've met yet. I'm Olivia, Ty's sister", she said as she offered her hand.

He replaced the lid to his water bottle and gave it a firm twist before wiping his free hand on his shorts. He then took a step toward her and shook her hand as he spoke. "Jarrod James. It's a pleasure..."

Olivia removed her hand from his grip and smiled. "How come I haven't seen you before?"

"Well, probably because I missed the latest poker game and I was out of town last weekend for the Halloween party."

"Oh. Well, are you sure you don't want just *one* doughnut? Surely one won't kill you!"

"No thanks." Jarrod turned away toward the refrigerator and reached for a cup that resembled the size of a bucket. He cracked five eggs into the cup, discarded the shells, and then added several dashes of hot sauce before raising it to his lips. He threw back his head and in one swift motion, swallowed the raw egg mixture. And as if his choice of breakfast was the most natural thing in the world, he simply rinsed his cup, turned around and headed back to the weight room.

The room fell silent for several moments before anyone spoke.

"Sweet baby Jesus", she whispered. "That brings a whole new meaning to sunny-side up, doesn't it?" The remaining men in the room suddenly broke out in laughter. She'd never seen anyone turn down one of Mr. Anderson's doughnuts before—and she'd certainly never witnessed consumption of a raw egg cocktail either. "Is the stove broke or something?"

And that's when she noticed. The entire kitchen looked different—newer. She'd been so caught up with visiting and then meeting Jarrod, she hadn't recognized there'd been a change. The avocado-green countertops had been replaced with black-speckled Formica; the outdated linoleum floor now covered with gray porcelain tile and the walls were painted a lighter shade of gray. The cabinets appeared to be the same, however they'd been painted white, brightening the once dull room.

She inquired about the renovations and was told that it'd taken place four years earlier. And the kitchen wasn't the only place to receive a facelift: the entire station had undergone one as well.

"If you'd like a tour, I can show you around", Grant offered.

"Thank you. That'd be great!"

They wound their way around the entire station: The bunk room where they slept, the "corral" that housed a row of black leather recliners and a wall-mounted T.V. for evening relaxation, the small weight room, and finally the bay where they'd stumbled upon one another earlier.

"So... Have you given any thought to my dinner invitation?"

Olivia bit her bottom lip and crossed her arms. "You are a persistent thing, aren't you?"

He studied her. She was clearly debating with herself.

Face it, Womack, she's not interested! "C'mon, you mean to tell me that the *'daredevil'* is afraid to have dinner with me?"

That sounded like a challenge... "Alright, what time?" she questioned.

"How about I pick you up at seven?"

"How about I meet you at your place at seven?" She countered.

Grant couldn't contain his smile. As usual, she needed to have the upper hand.

"Deal."

CHAPTER 5

Hmmm... a pair of jeans or a slinky dress?
It'd been over a year since her last date. Being a freelance photographer wasn't like other jobs. Natural and man-made disasters were never planned in advance. She couldn't glance at her schedule and predict when or where her next adventure would take her. Her frequent travels over the past year kept her far too busy for a relationship and after the horrific experience from her last date, she hadn't been overly eager to get back into the dating game.

Why are you obsessing over your wardrobe? This isn't a real date, remember? Grant is just a friend.

A friend who happens to kiss as though his life depended on it...

Olivia searched through her closet and finally decided on a long, navy maxi-dress, a fitted denim jacket, and a pair of silver sandals. The final ensemble was dressier than her normal everyday attire, yet still casual. She wanted to look nice, but she also didn't want to give Grant the impression that she'd put a lot of thought into tonight.

You have put a lot of thought into it—in fact, that's all you've been thinking about since you left the fire station yesterday!

Okay, so maybe she was a little excited. Was that so terrible?

Clearly they were attracted to one another and they had a good time whenever they were together. Their feelings for one another weren't serious—they were just having fun. It wasn't like she was going to sleep with him or anything—

"Where are you going tonight?" Ty asked as she approached the front door.

"Um, just having dinner with a friend."

She wasn't exactly sure why she'd said that. She wasn't sixteen; she was twenty-seven—an adult. He couldn't "forbid" her to have dinner with Grant. And besides, her and Grant were "friends." A man and a woman could have dinner together without labeling it a "date", couldn't they?

Raising the bottle to his lips, Grant took another large pull from his beer and then placed it on the counter. He hadn't planned on drinking before his date with Olivia, but as the minutes ticked by it became clear that he needed something to calm his nerves.

Quit acting like a fucking wuss! It's not even a real date—you practically dared her to have dinner with you...

Yeah, not one of his finest moments.

The doorbell rang, and after chugging the remainder of his beer, he hurried to open the door.

"Hey there, you ready?" she asked as she smiled.

"Wow. You look" —*good enough to eat*— "pretty."

Damn it, Womack, get your mind out of the gutter.

"Thank you. You clean up pretty nice yourself."

He couldn't help but stare. Her entire body was covered, the hem of her dress settled around her ankles; the denim jacket covered her arms. But he knew what existed beneath the material: a firm, yet feminine body. Visions of that mouthwatering figure, dressed in a skimpy referee costume, had haunted him for days. "Um... let me just grab my keys and we can—"

"—Oh, there's no need; I'm driving", she assured him confidently.

Scratching the stubble along his jaw, he studied her. "But you don't know where we're going."

"Not yet. But as soon as you tell me, I will", she countered playfully.

After closing the door behind him he took a step forward and reached for her hand. "Okay, I'm not going to argue with you. Let's get out of here."

Most of the small restaurants on the island were rather casual and inexpensive. The kind of places you'd expect to find a plastic checkered table-cloth, oversized booths, and a waitress that didn't hand you a menu because she already knew what you were going to order. But Grant didn't want to take Olivia to a place like that. He wanted to impress her.

They'd parked in the public lot and started down the boardwalk. "So now will you tell me where we're eatin'?" she asked impatiently.

Grant gestured toward the end of the pier. "I'm taking you to Snapper's."

"What...? Are you serious?"

"Of course, I'm serious..."

"I... I've never been there before—I've always wanted to, though."

Reaching for her hand, he raised it to his lips and kissed the soft skin along the back. "Well then, I guess tonight is your lucky night..."

They were seated outside along the pier overlooking a fiery sunset, listening to the gentle waves collide against the wood pilings beneath. The subtle coastal breeze on a determined voyage to reach land.

He observed as Olivia unfolded her white cloth napkin and placed it gently in her lap. "I hope this table is okay."

"This is perfect, Grant... Thank you."

"You're welcome."

They ordered a bottle of red wine and enjoyed a tray of oysters on the half shell before their entrees arrived. The wind was beginning to pick up as the sun fulfilled its destiny and he couldn't seem to peel his eyes away from her as the gulf breeze gently tousled her honey-blonde locks. Her countless attempts to tuck her hair behind her ear, only to be disturbed by the wind again, fascinating him.

It was strangely... *erotic*. In fact, his fingers were practically twitching at the thought of tangling them in her hair.

Damn it, Womack, what the hell's the matter with you?

Well, wasn't that the million dollar question? Every simple, nonchalant thing she did somehow turned him on: her hair blowing in the breeze, the way she stuck her pinky finger out when she took a sip of wine, the way she licked those pouty pink lips—

"Kendall told me you're Mr. Gibson's grandson. How come I never remember you comin' to visit him?"

"Probably because I didn't."

"Oh. Is that because you lived far away?" she asked as she dipped her bread into the clam sauce at the bottom of her bowl.

"No. I grew up in Pensacola." He took a sip of his wine, debating about how much detail he wanted to go into about his past. It wasn't something he talked about regularly, but somehow it seemed easy to open up to her. Maybe it was the adorable southern accent. Or maybe it was the intensity behind those emerald eyes, delivering a message of comfort and understanding.

"My grandpa and my parents didn't get along. They weren't on speaking terms when he died five years ago..."

Olivia reached out and grabbed his hand across the table and gave it a squeeze. "I'm so sorry", she uttered softly.

"It's okay." God, she was so beautiful, her eyes reflecting concern and recognition. She understood the loss of a loved one probably better than anyone he'd ever met and before he even realized it, he was speaking again. "My parents and my grandpa had a *'disagreement'* when I was just a baby. And in an attempt to punish him, my parents refused to let him see me. About six years ago, right before he died, I came here and spent a week with him..."

Sensing the somber aura, Olivia decided to share one of her fondest memories of Grant's grandpa, one that would not only transform the sudden doleful mood, but also acquaint him with the kind of man his grandpa was.

"Mr. Gibson was probably the most genuine person I've ever had the pleasure of knowin'. When I was a little girl and Ty would take me to the beach, your grandpa would sit out on the back deck, and on really hot days, he'd come down the steps and bring us some sweet tea. He made the best sweet tea I've ever tasted."

Grant chuckled. "Yeah, he sure did... so anyway, enough about me. I want to know about you."

Olivia's posture stiffened slightly. "Well, there's not much to tell, really. I moved here with Ty when I was nine after my parents died; left the island for college two days after I graduated and never came back until now."

"Where'd you go to college?"

"A small arts college in Northern Louisiana. I studied photography."

Grant took another sip of wine and then placed his glass gently in front of him on the table. He studied her for a long beat, her disposition softening before him. "Ty tells me you're a freelance photographer."

"Uh-huh. Three months after I graduated college, Hurricane Katrina hit. After the storm I packed my camera and took pictures of some of the aftermath. I hadn't planned on specializin' in any particular kind of photography, but that experience changed me."

Stroking the stubble along his pronounced jaw, his eyes bored into hers. "How do you mean?" he asked curiously.

"Well, most folks heard about the storm and probably thought it was such an unfortunate thing to happen and then went on with their everyday lives... There was so much devastation, Grant—I mean parts of the city looked like it was a part of a third world country! So many people lost everything they had and for most of them that wasn't much. For me capturing pictures of the devastation and chaos after the storm was like speakin' for those who didn't have a voice. My pictures helped New Orleans command the national attention that it so desperately needed."

He loved how her features lit up whenever she spoke about her career. He was beginning to see a whole new side of her—a caring, softer side. And he liked it.

After dinner they took a lazy stroll down the boardwalk and turned the corner toward the part of the pier that ran parallel to the shore. Darkness blanketed the night sky, the stars glistening like diamonds amongst a mine of black coal. Up ahead the historic Ferris wheel towered above the pier, gliding effortlessly like a pirouetting ballerina.

Their date was coming to an end, but not before he stole a private moment away with her on the Ferris wheel. Grant gestured toward the ride, "That's where we're headed next."

Olivia came to an abrupt halt. "Whoa—wait a minute. You said dinner; you never mentioned anything about a Ferris wheel..."

He turned to face her, reaching for her hand. "Technically you're correct, but now that we're here..."

She tried to contain her nerves. She was terrified of heights. It was probably ridiculous considering
all of the dangerous and crazy behavior that'd cluttered her past. She could feel her palms becoming
slick, could hear her rapid pulse in her ears. Her
body's fight or flight mechanism was set into motion.
More than anything she wanted to gather the bottom
of her dress and sprint toward her car, but she knew
she couldn't.

He glanced at their joined hands. "You okay?"
he asked. "You're hands are shaking."

"It's j-just the wind. It's getting c-cooler out
here", she stuttered.

Grant raked his eyes over her body. She was
trembling, her hands were clammy, and her pupils
were dilated. And suddenly he had an epiphany.
"You're scared."

"*What?*"

Now her face flushed a brilliant shade of red.
"You are, aren't you...? You're *really scared* right now!"

"Don't be ridiculous!" she countered. "It's just..."

Grant licked his lips and grinned. "Children
get on, you know—even frail old ladies."

"What's your point, Womack?"

"The point is, I think I've stumbled across the
one thing that the 'daredevil' is afraid of", he uttered
as he gestured with his index finger.

Olivia lunged forward and placed her palm
over his mouth. "Shhh! Do you mind keepin' your
voice down? Nobody on the island needs to know that
heights make me... uncomfortable."

Uncomfortable... Her choice of words didn't
surprise him. No way was she going to admit she was
scared! Grant grabbed her wrist, rotating it in order

to plant a kiss on the back of her hand. If she only knew how incredibly adorable and irresistible she looked. "Well, *DD,* I think it's time to conquer your fear. What do you say?"

Are you nuts, girl? Grant "GQ" Womack exposes a bone-melting smile and you're putty in his large, manly hands!

Alright, so if not for his charming good looks, she probably would have told him to go to hell. But honestly—she couldn't think of a more perfect person to take this journey with her.

"Okay", she said hesitantly, "but let me make something perfectly clear: If it weren't for the fact that you helped me after my jellyfish incident, I'd tell you where you could shove that Ferris wheel right now..."

He took a step closer, lifting her chin with his fingertips; savoring the genuine smile adorned to her beautiful face. "Point taken."

"Good."

Slowly, they walked toward the Ferris wheel, her heart threatening to burst with every step she took. The ride was nearly empty, no eager customers waiting in line.

Yeah, probably because you're the only one stupid enough to get talked into falling one hundred fifty feet to your death!

She watched as Grant handed the ride attendant two tickets and then whispered something in the man's ear. The young man smiled and nodded and as the next bucket seat approached, he ushered them inside and lowered the bar snug across their lap.

Just breathe. You can do this, girl... "Can I ask you a question?"

"Anything", he answered.

"What did you whisper to the ride attendant before we climbed aboard?"

Grant hesitated for a moment. "I told him... this was your first ride; to go easy on you—"

Suddenly the ride jerked into motion, causing the bucket to sway back and forth; also causing a strangled squeal to escape from the back of Olivia's throat. She clenched her eyes shut, dug her nails into his arm and leaned into him.

Humpty dumpty sat on a wall.

Humpty dumpty had a great fall...

"Jesus, Joseph and Mary—how long is this gonna take?" she uttered breathlessly.

"Open your eyes", he said as they continued to climb.

"I can't!"

Without warning the ride came to an abrupt halt, forcing the bucket into another terrifying shift. Another soft squeal escaped her lips, her eyes still closed, her arms clamped around his like a vice. "Why are we stoppin'? Are we done yet?" she asked, her voice shuddering with fear.

"No, we're at the top—"

"Are you kidding me? Why on God's green earth would he stop us at the top?"

"Relax. He's probably letting someone on or off the ride. We'll start moving again in a minute", he explained.

All the king's horses and all the king's men

Couldn't put humpty dumpty back together again.

Olivia waited a few moments. "Geez, how long does it take to exit the ride? Why aren't we movin'?"

"Open your eyes—you can see the entire island

from up here", he suggested, doing his best to distract her and avoid the question.

"No, that's alright. I'm quite fine with my eyes shut, thank you very much. And why are you avoiding my question?"

Busted. Scratching the stubble along his chin he asked, "I'm sorry—what was the question again?"

"Why aren't we moving? Are we stuck?" she asked again.

Grant chuckled under his breath and smiled. She looked so adorable with her eyes clenched, latching onto his arm with a strong, desperate grip. He leaned his head toward hers and positioned his mouth inches away from her ear when he finally spoke. "Open your eyes and then I'll answer the question", he whispered.

"Are you trying to torture me? Because if so, you're doing one hell of a job!"

"Just humor me, okay? Open your eyes..."

Olivia took a deep breath and opened one of her eyes, aware that Grant was staring back at her, obviously amused by her reluctance. "Okay, there."

"Huh-uh", he uttered. "Both of them..."

She blew out a puff of air in frustration and finally gathered the courage to open it. No longer afraid to show the level of anxiety she was experiencing, she asked again. "Why aren't we moving? Are we stuck?"

The sincerity in her voice twisted his insides. He really hadn't meant to cause her any unnecessary anguish; he'd only wanted to steal a few private, unforgettable moments away with her. Her emerald eyes were ironically transparent, revealing how cumbersome the situation was to her. She was frightened and maybe even a little embarrassed at her loss of control—obviously something she didn't experience often.

Alright, Womack, time to come clean...

"Not exactly", he explained.

"What is *that* supposed to mean?" Feeling a wave of hysteria crash over her, she buried her distraught face in her hands. "Oh, this is no good! We're gonna have to climb down, aren't we? Darn it, I knew I should've kept my feet on solid ground—what the hell was I thinkin'?—"

"—Relax, Livvy... I paid the ride attendant to give us some privacy for a few minutes."

"What did you say?" she asked as she removed her hands from her face and met his gaze.

"I wanted us to have some privacy. So I paid the guy to—"

"No—not that. What did you just call me?"

Shit, now you're totally fucked! Way to go, Casanova—you probably said another girl's name... "Um... *Olivia?*"

"No, that's not what you said. You called me *Livvy*. That's... that's what my parents used to call me..."

"I'm sorry. I didn't—"

"No—it's okay. Nobody knows that..." She stared into his apologetic eyes, the ice-blue hue suddenly warming with desire.

"So, you're not mad then?" he asked for confirmation. Olivia shook her head slowly from side-to-side, her gaze never leaving his. "Good. Close your eyes", he whispered.

"Now you want me to close them?" she asked in disbelief.

"Uh-huh."

"My pleasure." Olivia closed her eyes and felt his fingertips gently lift her chin upward.

Grant closed the distance between them, his heart pounding, and his mind empty except for the overwhelming urge to feel her lips against his again. The kiss started slow and controlled, but moments after it began his restraint failed him. She tasted sinfully sweet—almost too good—and with every lustful stroke of her slick tongue, he could feel her fear subside.

She was gone... in the moment—*in him.* Their tongues waltzed in unison, finding a rhythm that was both emphatic and beautiful. As their appetite for one another increased, the cadence of their colliding tongues became rapid and powerful.

He tangled his hands in her hair, his fingers gently tugging her honey-blonde locks, appreciative for the opportunity to finally coil it around them like he'd wanted to do earlier during dinner. He angled her head in an effort to deepen the kiss and heard an encouraging moan escape from the back of her throat.

The sound was unmistakable... She was enjoying it just as much as he was.

Suddenly he felt as though he couldn't get close enough. He wanted her. Wanted to explore her petite body with his hands; caress her gentle curves like a priceless, sculpted piece of art.

Nothing mattered except for this—not her apartment back in New Orleans, her photography career, *the fact that she was currently suspended one hundred fifty feet in the air*... nothing. For the first time in her life, her mind was blank. There were no to-do lists, no horrid or painful memories haunting her. There was just the intoxicating taste and sensation of Grant.

Her sounds reverberated through his body, igniting a hunger he'd never unleashed. He disentangled his hands from her hair and trailed his fingertips down her spine. When he reached her bottom he grabbed a hold and held on for life. Feeling as though he'd die if he didn't get closer, he shifted his weight, attempting to turn his body toward her. But his swift modification had unforeseen consequences. His sudden movement mobilized the bucket as well, causing it to sway again.

Olivia tore her mouth away from his and gripped his shirt in both of her hands. "Don't ever do that again!" she shouted.

"What?—you mean kiss you?" he asked breathlessly.

A sexy smile spread across her wet, swollen lips. "No—*you can do that*. I meant don't rock the seat."

"Got it."

He leaned toward her, attempting to taste her lips again, but before he had the chance the ride jerked into motion. Her eyes clenched and her grip strengthened as they descended.

Careful, Womack, that sensation in the pit of your gut isn't from your descent.

Yeah, he needed to be careful. Falling for his best friend's little sister could only end badly...

CHAPTER 6

The sun was desperately trying to stake its claim in the late morning sky, but the thick blanket of murky, gray clouds shielded much of its brilliance thus far. The clouds were gracefully moving north toward the mainland, indicating that the sun would soon prevail.

Olivia sauntered toward the mailbox. Before she'd left New Orleans she'd completed the necessary paperwork to have her mail forwarded to Butler Island. At the time she wasn't certain how long she'd be out of town. It wasn't unusual for a week's worth of mail to clutter her mailbox back home. She traveled out of town often; sometimes leaving on a moment's notice. But her spur-of-the-moment return to the island was going to keep her away much longer than a week. In fact, she'd already been here for almost three weeks and her departure date had yet to be determined.

After opening the small metal door, she acquired the paper contents inside, sorting through them until she came upon a manila envelope from Adversity Magazine. She tucked the remaining mail under her arm and then slid her index finger under the fold to pry the package open. Inside she discovered an advanced copy of next month's magazine, one of her photographs printed on the cover.

The picture had been taken three weeks before she'd returned to Butler Island. She'd traveled to Washington State to capture damage from a 5.0 magnitude earthquake that'd struck the area surrounding Mount Rainier. The photograph had captured a group of scientists kneeling in front of a broken segment of road, studying the damage near the base of the volcano, the majestic mountain's snow-capped peak visible in the background.

Olivia reached into the manila envelope and unveiled a sizeable check for the use of her photograph. This wasn't the first time one of her photos had made the cover of Adversity Magazine, but it was the first time she'd been rewarded a check with that many zeros. Apparently the magazine was beginning to appreciate her unique perspective, her freelance compensation proof of her hard work and talent.

Photography had always been rewarding—not always monetarily—but personally. She loved capturing moments in time through the lens of her camera, sharing her perspective anonymously through her still shots. It still amazed her that photographs could evoke such emotion—without sound or movement: anger, inspiration, empathy. Sorrow. Illustrating catastrophe in current events was only part of the job—extracting emotion from the person viewing her work was of utmost importance.

Since her return to the small island, she hadn't

captured many shots. But that was soon going to change. She needed to speak with Chief Handler and ask permission to accompany the firefighters on future calls. Most likely she'd only capture the rescue of the occasional stranded cat in a tree. But on the off-chance that another *"suspicious"* fire broke out, she wanted to be prepared.

The sun was finally beginning to win its battle with the murky clouds, its warm radiance glaring upon her skin. After quickly heading inside, she reached for her camera and her keys. Her destination: the beach. The jellyfish encounter robbed her of the opportunity to capture still shots of the powdery sand, clear gulf water, and the hypnotic horizon several weeks ago and with the clouds finally dissipating, a quiet afternoon with her camera at the beach was long overdue.

Raising his forearm to his brow, Grant wiped a bead of sweat away. He'd been sanding the exterior siding of his beach house for most of the morning, preparing the wood for a fresh coat of paint. He'd inherited the home after his grandpa died five years earlier. Over the years he'd made improvements to the interior: painted the walls, refinished the hardwood floors, and updated the kitchen and bathrooms. But he'd saved the dull, lackluster exterior for last.

Grandpa Gibson was eighty-four when he passed, his frail frame unable to manage the upkeep of his beloved home any longer. When Grant had first moved-in, the task of restoring the historical stilt-home seemed daunting. He'd been so overwhelmed. After the initial shock had subsided, he'd set a plan into motion and little by little, transformed his inheritance into his personal coastal sanctuary.

The radiant sun chased the remaining dismal clouds from the sky, casting its warm, rejuvenating rays upon his bare back. A break from his hard work was long overdue. After tossing his sandpaper into his toolbox, he sauntered inside, grabbed a beer from the fridge, and then returned to the deck. He sat at the patio table and then took a pull from his beer, scanning the horizon.

He hadn't been able to get his date with Olivia out of his mind. It was by far his best first date ever. He'd learned a lot about her and had even shared a glimpse of his past—something he didn't do very often. In fact, come to think of it… that was a first for him, too.

The Ferris wheel ride couldn't have gone better either. She'd been terrified, but had trusted him. Olivia stared fear in the eyes, refusing to let it cripple her and observing it had fascinated him. Hell, who was he kidding?—everything she did fascinated him! He'd thoroughly enjoyed their kiss and judging by her erotic moans, she had as well.

After they'd left the boardwalk she'd driven him home. He'd kissed her goodbye—this time with more control and restraint—and before he'd exited the car, she'd promised she'd call…

That was four days ago.

He'd carried his cell phone with him everywhere, afraid he'd miss her call. He even dialed her number a time or two—*okay, more than a time or two*—but had always hesitated to press the final digit. *She'd* said *she* would call. Maybe he was just overreacting? Maybe she'd been busy…

Yeah, that was probably it. She was probably organizing her closets or...

Listen to yourself, Womack. You sound fucking pathetic! She's been busy alright—busy avoiding you!

Yeah, he was afraid of that. Because for the very first time in his adult life, he'd walked away from a first date desperately wanting another.

Grant took another pull from his beer and froze when his eyes landed on a familiar image: a black Mini Cooper parked approximately one hundred feet to his left in the adjacent public lot. He placed his beer on the patio table and then stood, scanning the beach in search of the owner. He finally spotted her, attaching her camera to a tri-pod not far from her parked car.

He glanced toward the deck railing where his chocolate lab was lazily lounging and then smacked the side of his thigh several times to get his attention. "Come here, boy", he instructed. When the dog leapt toward him, he knelt down and gave his companion a satisfying scratch behind the ears and in return, he received a sloppy, wet lick to the cheek.

"You see that girl over there, boy?" he asked as he pointed in Olivia's direction. "I've got a nice, juicy treat with your name written all over it. All you have to do is run over there and let her pet you. What do ya say?"

The dog answered with two loud barks, communicating his understanding. "Alright, boy, go get her!"

Without hesitation, the dog hurried down the wooden steps and took off toward her direction. Grant waited several seconds and then followed suit.

By the time he reached them, Olivia had already knelt down and was running her soft fingertips along Dexter's neck. His dog appeared to be in a state of pure bliss.

Damned lucky dog—what he wouldn't give to trade places with him right now...

"Hey", he called out. "Sorry about that!"

"It's okay! He yours?" she asked.

"Yes ma'am."

"I didn't know you had a dog. Where was he when you were fixin' up my foot a couple weeks ago?"

"Probably inside napping."

"Oh. What's his name?"

"Dexter." Grant whistled and jerked his head back toward the beach house. "Dexter, go home!" he instructed. Happy to please his owner—and secure his promised treat—Dexter pulled away from Olivia's grip and raced back toward the deck.

"He's beautiful", she said as she watched him run away.

So are you... "Thanks." He gestured toward the equipment behind her. "That's a fancy-looking camera you have there."

"This is my pride and joy—I bought it a few months ago. Do me a favor, will you?" Olivia pointed to the area in front of the camera. "Stand right over there."

Grant shook his head and crossed his arms. "Oh, no—I don't do pictures."

Placing one of her hands on her hip, she tilted her head to the side. "Oh c'mon, it's just a test shot. I need to adjust my focus—I promise I won't make you do any silly poses. *Please...*?" she asked as she innocently batted her long lashes at him.

Grant slowly ambled in front of the camera, rubbing the stubble along his jaw. "Here?" he asked.

"Uh-huh, now turn and face me."

She waited until he complied and then began fidgeting with her camera lens. Grant stood in front of her, shirtless, with his hands shoved into his front pockets, his faded denim jeans sitting low on his hips. Her eyes swept along his sleeve tattoo, down his broad, toned chest, his rippled six-pack abs and finally ended at the dark trail of hair that disappeared behind the fly of his jeans.

Oh. My. God.

His body was certainly a temple—*one that she was thoroughly worshiping at the moment.*

"Can you back up a little...?" she asked. "A little more." Still facing the camera he stepped backward, his feet only inches away from the water's edge.

And suddenly, she had an idea...

She turned on the camera's time-lapse feature, allowing her to automatically capture a picture every five seconds over the course of one minute. Adjusting the focus one last time, she instructed him to take one large step back...

Grant complied with her last request, so mesmerized by how beautiful she looked in those tiny cut-off denim shorts that he hadn't noticed how close he'd been to the water's edge. He'd taken a large step back and had ended up in the ocean, the chilly gulf water saturating his denim jeans midway up his lower legs.

"Whoops!" she called out sarcastically.

Grant glanced at his submerged feet and then focused his attention back on Olivia, who was guiltlessly smiling back at him. "Oh, you think that's funny, do you?"

"Uh-huh", she finally answered, biting her bottom lip to suppress her mischievous grin.

"Oh—you're gonna pay for that one!" he shouted as he lunged toward her.

A playful squeal escaped as she tried to dodge him, but he was too quick. He grabbed her by the waist, pulling the back of her fleeing body against the hard plane of his chest and then lifted her feet off the ground as though she weighed nothing. She struggled to set herself free, but his grip was firm and she was weak from laughter.

Walking toward the shore, Grant waded in the chilly water while Olivia playfully squirmed in his arms, the sound of her laughter provoking his. He quickly repositioned her in his arms so that he was supporting her upper body and the back of her legs.

"Grant!" she cried. "Put me down!"

With the waves gently colliding against his knees, he met her gaze, mirroring the mischievous grin she'd given him moments earlier.

"Oh, no! *Wait*—"

But it was too late. He'd loosened his grip, carefully tossing her into the frigid gulf as though he was freeing a fish he'd caught. A high-pitched scream escaped her lips, followed by a loud gasp as her body sunk beneath the surface.

"You made me all wet!" she shouted breathlessly.

Smiling seductively, he offered her his hand. "Ah, the words every man longs to hear..."

"Okay, first you torture me with a Ferris wheel ride and now you throw me in the ocean—the *very cold* ocean. I think I'm finally beginnin' to understand why you're still single!"

After accepting his hand, he helped her up. "Boys always pick on the girls they like, you know."

"Is that so?" she asked as she walked behind him, her fingertips trailing up his tattooed arm, over his broad shoulder, and eventually gliding down his muscular back.

Grant closed his eyes, relishing the sensation. "Uh-huh", he finally managed.

Satisfied that he was distracted, her fingers continued exploring his back. "Are you ready, Grant?" she asked, her voice filled with desire.

Hell yeah, he was ready; ready to use his fingers on her—in her.

"Ready for what?" he questioned, deciphering whether or not they were on the same page.

Olivia brushed her lips along his back. "Ready to fall for me", she mumbled.

Finally in a position to seek revenge, she swiftly shoved her foot along the back of his knee, causing his six-foot muscular frame to collapse into the shivery water; *"falling"* as she'd intended for him to do.

"Damn, that's cold!" he cried. His quick reflexes landed him promptly back on his feet again; pivoting, he met her gaze. "Alright, I guess we're even now."

"Y-yeah, I think s-so", she managed as she hugged herself for warmth. She watched in amazement as rivulets of frigid salt water descended down his powerful chest and rippled torso. Good heavens—the man was built like a Greek God!

Grant took a step toward her, placing his large callused hands on her upper arms. "We need to get you warm. C'mon, I'll make a pot of coffee and get you a towel."

Wading through the water toward the shore, they gathered her equipment and then shuffled their bare feet through the velvety sand. After reaching the beach house, they rinsed their feet and then quickly covered themselves with two extra-large beach towels.

"Take off your clothes", he demanded.

"Excuse me?" She asked in disbelief.

"I've got a dry change of clothes you can put on. Unless, of course, you *want* to sit out here naked..."

Olivia smiled. "No, I don't suppose that would be a good idea." After rising from the lounge chair she started toward the sliding glass door.

"Down the hall, first door on your left. By the time you get back the coffee should be ready."

"Okay, thank you."

While the coffee brewed, Grant removed his wet clothes and changed into a dry pair of jeans and a plain white t-shirt. Before heading back to the deck, he stopped in front of the guest bathroom and knocked on the door. "Everything okay?" he asked.

"I'm fine", she responded from the other side.

"How do you take your coffee?"

"Plenty of cream; a lil' sugar."

Olivia took off her water-logged wardrobe and lifted a flannel shirt off the counter that he'd left. She slipped her arms into the soft material, inhaling the aroma from his laundry soap, and then quickly fastened the garment.

What are you doing, girl?

Wasn't *that* the million dollar question? The truth was, she didn't have a clue. Staying here was probably the worst idea ever. She needed to go. They'd had their fun on the beach and now she needed to get far, far away from him. This friendship, this—whatever it was—was supposed to be all in the name of *fun*.

An adventure. Something light and easy and... well, *fun*. Watching him chase after her was fun.

But what would happen when he finally caught her...?

After glancing in the mirror, she tousled her hair with her fingertips and then retraced her steps back to the deck. Her intention: explain that she really needed to head home. But one look at the arrangement he'd set-up changed everything. Grant was standing with his back turned, tending to the fire in the portable black fire pit. He'd already hauled the outdoor patio loveseat closer to the flames, and had even draped a large Afghan over the cushion for added warmth.

Okay, so maybe she could stay for just one cup of coffee...

Olivia opened the sliding glass door and stepped onto the wooden deck. "I think somebody has a guilty conscience."

"Wow!" he uttered as he glanced over his shoulder. The flannel shirt fell just below mid-thigh, revealing the sexiest pair of legs he'd ever seen. "You look... *wow*", he repeated. "I had no idea a flannel shirt could look so good."

Taking a seat, she covered her bare legs with the Afghan and reached for the cup of coffee sitting next to her on the adjacent table. "Flatterin' will get you nowhere, Womack."

Grant laughed softly, revealing that trademark grin he'd perfected. After he was comfortable with the size of the flames, he joined her on the loveseat.

"This is really nice. You sit out here a lot?" she asked.

"Yeah, I spend most of my time out here."

"Well, I can see why." Olivia palmed the side of her coffee mug with both hands, her icy fingers slowly absorbing the residual heat.

The wind was gaining momentum, gently blowing her blonde locks and before he could stop himself, his fingers twirled around a small segment near her ear. Shifting in his seat, he turned toward her. It was still slightly damp from their earlier plunge. "Your hair is so soft."

Uh-oh. "Thank you."

"You're so beautiful—everything about you", he murmured, his gravelly voice saturated with desire.

Olivia swallowed hard. "I'm sure you say that to all the girls you bring home."

"Huh-uh", he uttered. "I don't usually bring dates back to my place." He released her hair and cupped the back of her neck, his other hand grazing the afghan over her lap. Pressing his warm lips against the soft skin along her neck, he mumbled, "What are your plans tomorrow night?"

God he felt good. It was like he owned the instruction manual to her body. He knew where she wanted to be touched; how she wanted to be touched. Her eyes drifted shut as his lips migrated toward the sensitive area just below her ear. "I don't know. It depends, I guess", she whispered.

"Depends on..."

Olivia tilted her head to the right slightly, giving him better access. "What are ya offering?"

"Well, I had a good time the other night. I was hoping we could do dinner again... *here.*"

"I thought you were working tomorrow."

"I am."

Olivia placed her hand against his chest and gently pushed him back so that she could look at him. "I'm confused. If you're working tomorrow, how are we gonna have dinner here?"

Tucking a strand of hair behind one of her ears, he answered, "I don't work twenty-four hour shifts anymore."

"I don't understand—Ty does."

"That's because he's a lieutenant. Last year the city was having a budget crisis. They were looking to eliminate four firefighter positions and three at the police station. So to prevent lay-offs, we all bound together and came up with a solution: work twelve hour shifts. Everyone pretty much agreed that cutting back our salary was better than no salary at all."

"Okay, so, what happens if there's an emergency after seven o'clock?" she challenged.

"Well, in the evenings I'm on call."

"On call..."

"Yeah, we all have an on-call phone. When we're needed, dispatch alerts us and then we either head back to the station, or meet the fire engine at the determined destination."

"Oh. I guess that's why the bunk room looked like a ghost town when I visited the station last week."

Grant nodded in agreement. "So about dinner..."

Staring into her coffee cup, she smiled. "You just don't give up, do you?"

"Not when I see something I want..."

Olivia gnawed on her bottom lip for a moment.

This is a bad idea, girl.

Yeah, she was aware of that—their chemistry was on the verge of combusting. Having dinner wasn't necessarily the issue. Her concern was what came after. But somehow, telling him no didn't sit right with her either.

They had *fun*. So what if they acted on their mutual attraction? She wasn't going to sleep with him—she didn't participate in casual sex. Control was her middle name.

No way was she going to lose it.

Surely she could stay in control *and* still have fun...

"What time?"

CHAPTER 7

Clutching a bottle of pinot noir, Olivia raised her free hand and firmly knocked on the front door. She inhaled a deep, calming breath and then slowly exhaled. She'd had reservations about tonight. Yes, it was just dinner. But she was beginning to see a pattern: every time she was around Grant she tended to lose her self-control. It was like the pleasure side of her brain overpowered the logical side.

She'd been so indecisive about tonight. Numerous times she'd dialed his number to cancel, but hesitated.

Why? Well, unfortunately that was an easy question to answer: He showed a genuine interest in getting to know her—the real her.

And the fact that his lips ignite an internal inferno had nothing to do with it?

Okay, so that probably played a role in her decision to keep their dinner plans, too. But, damn it, tonight she was going to practice some restraint. The logical side of her brain had to remain in charge

because if she lost control again, she was in big
trouble.

"Hey, beautiful", he said as he answered the
door, although "beautiful" couldn't even begin to describe how amazing she looked. She wore a deep green
blouse that buttoned down the front, mirroring the
intensity from her emerald eyes. A pair of black jeans
hugged her soft curves, daring his eyes to trace her
sensual silhouette. Stepping forward, he wrapped his
arms around her narrow waist, filling his lungs with
the scent of her floral shampoo.

"I hope I'm not late", she said as she gently
leaned into him.

"Nope—you're right on time."

After their embrace, Olivia followed Grant inside. He took the bottle of wine from her grasp and
moved into the kitchen to open it.

"So what are you makin'?" she asked.

"It's a surprise", he answered as he filled her
wine glass.

"Oh?"

Walking toward her, he offered her one of the
glasses. "That's right." His fingers tucked a strand of
hair behind one of her ears and then gently tilted her
chin upward. He gave her a quick peck on the lips
and then pulled back to look at her. "I just have a
couple of things left to do. Why don't you take your
glass of wine out on the deck and I'll be out there in a
few minutes to join you."

Olivia eyed him suspiciously. "What are you up
to, Womack?"

"I guess you're gonna have to just trust me."

"Trust *you?*" she questioned sarcastically. "You
mean the same guy that tossed me in the ocean

yesterday?—*that guy?*"

Opening the sliding glass door, Grant smiled at her. "Yeah, that's the one."

After the door was shut behind her, she leisurely walked to the edge of the deck and leaned her elbows along the railing. The sun had just disappeared to her right, leaving vibrant hues of pink, orange, and lavender in its wake. Up ahead, the tide was steadily rising, the brisk water devouring the soft, velvety sand with every mellow wave.

Olivia took a sip of wine and then focused her attention on the docile chocolate lab brushing against her thigh.

"Hey, Dexter!" she exclaimed as she knelt down to pet him. With his tail wagging like a pair of windshield wipers during a monsoon, he stepped closer and then lapped her cheek with his tongue.

"Should I be jealous?" Grant asked as he emerged from the kitchen.

Olivia glanced over her shoulder while she scratched along Dexter's neck. "Perhaps you should be. This handsome devil right here would never toss a lady in the ocean. Would ya, boy?"

Dexter responded by giving her cheek another sloppy lick.

"In case you forgot, *you* started it", he reminded her. "I should've known you were up to no good!"

Olivia revealed a mischievous grin and then stood up.

"Dexter", he called, "go lie down!" The dog trotted to the corner of the deck, turned two complete circles, and then lowered his body onto a navy-blue cushion.

"Wow! He listens really well!"

"Yeah, he's a good dog... Um, go ahead and have a seat. Dinner's ready."

Olivia settled into the chair he'd offered, her eyes focused on the lone hurricane lamp in the center of the table. Grant disappeared into the kitchen and then returned moments later carrying a large platter with several dishes balanced on top. When he placed her bowl in front of her, she quickly turned her head to meet his gaze. "Shrimp and grits...? You made me shrimp and grits?" she questioned in disbelief.

"Yeah, probably not as good as what you'd find in New Orleans, but—"

"Grant, this is my *favorite!* How did you know?"

After placing his bowl on the table, he took the seat beside her. "I called Kendall."

The corners of her mouth ascended into a wide grin. "Look at you, trying to impress me."

"Is it working?"

"Maybe..."

Conversation was fairly lighthearted during dinner. She complimented him on a job well-done, explaining that if she couldn't be in New Orleans, his rendition of shrimp and grits was the next best thing. Having heard about her famous grits, he'd asked for some pointers and she'd jokingly responded that if she shared her secret, she'd have to kill him. But when their bowls were finally empty, their conversation veered away from playful.

"So you've lived in New Orleans for how long?"

"Well, I visited right after Hurricane Katrina. I spent a couple of weeks there documentin' the clean-up efforts and then headed back to my apartment upstate for a few days. But it just didn't feel right, ya know?"

Grant studied her for a long beat. "What do you mean?"

"Have you ever been there?" she asked. When he shook his head indicating that he hadn't, she went on. "I don't know. There's this... *vibe* in New Orleans. I've traveled all over the country for my career and I've never felt anything like it anywhere else."

Running the back of his fingers across the short stubble along his jaw, he pinned her with his eyes. "What does it feel like?"

"Like... like I'm *alive*."

Grant reached out and placed the pads of his middle and index fingers over the pulse point on the inside of her wrist and smirked. "Well, I guess there's no need to go back then. You feel alive to me."

Olivia laughed and then slid her arm away from his grasp. "I'm not sure if I told you the other day, but the house is lookin' really great."

"Thanks—it's been a work in-progress for a few years now."

"Really?"

"Uh-huh." Throwing his head back, he emptied the last bit of wine from his glass and then gently placed it in front of him on the wrought-iron patio table. "My grandpa was... well he was really old. He had a hard time with the upkeep. About six years ago, before he died, I came to visit him. I did as much as I could for him during the week I was here, but..."

His brows furrowed, revealing a glimpse of the overwhelming pain and regret he'd kept hidden so well. He was denied a relationship with his grandpa over a dispute his parents had had with Mr. Gibson when he was just a boy. He'd attempted to bridge that gap six years ago and had managed to build a very special bond with his grandpa in a limited amount of time, yet still held himself partly responsible for not having known him better. Olivia covered his hand with hers and gave it a firm squeeze. "I think your grandpa would be really proud of what you've done with the place."

Grant looked at their joined hands and then focused his attention on the gorgeous woman sitting next to him. He was almost speechless—she never ceased to amaze him. He hadn't meant to unveil his remorse. She made him open up about things he'd never shared with anyone—*made him feel things he'd never felt before.* "You're almost too good to be real", he uttered softly.

"You wanna check my pulse again? I can as-sure you I'm quite real!"

A powerful gust of wind washed over them, but neither seemed to notice. His eye's bored into hers, searching. Searching for clues; some sort of sign that indicated she was feeling the same way he was. His attention was temporarily diverted to her mouth as she raked her teeth across the surface of her pouty bottom lip. She was completely unaware how erotic that simple action was, but he certainly wasn't.

Something was definitely happening here, she acknowledged. Their bodies were communicating—sending and receiving messages—longing for the opportunity to take action.

Stay in control!

She needed to intercept these messages; needed to keep things light and easy. She closed the distance between them; could see him lick his lips in anticipation. When she was mere inches from his mouth his lips parted, inviting her to lose herself in his testosterone-laced kiss.

Not so fast, Womack.

At the last moment, she turned her head slightly and pressed her lips against the side of his cheek.

Yes, this kind of made her a bit of a tease. But she desperately needed to stand her ground. She needed to set boundaries. Flirting was fun and playful and an occasional kiss here and there was fine. But that was as far as this "thing" between them could go.

"Thank you for dinner. It was delicious", she whispered. She started to pull away, but one of his hands reached up and cupped the back of her neck, preventing her from fleeing. He aligned their mouths, regaining control and stealing what small amount of will power she had left. She could feel his warm breath against her lips and inhaled the intoxicating spice. And just as she felt the first hint of his eager lips brush against hers, she felt something else—

Raindrops.

Several oversized drops collided against her skin, landing on her cheek with a heavy thud; warning that there was an army of raindrops prepared to plummet after. She felt Grant smile against her mouth as the quantity of drops increased and when it became clear that the intensity would only continue to grow, they both leapt from their seats, laughing as they collected their empty bowls.

They managed to open the sliding glass door, seeking shelter inside just as the sky released a blanket of water from the saturated clouds hovering above. Once inside, Dexter vigorously shook his body, ridding his chocolate coat of excess water, inadvertently dousing the two of them.

"Where in the hell did all that come from?" he asked as he swept his hand through the air, gesturing toward the wall of water assaulting the patio.

"I don't know!"

Grant took her empty bowl and walked toward the sink.

"If I didn't know better, I'd have thought you were trying to get me wet again—"

Holy shit!

Grant lost his grip. The dishes tumbled, clashing together like an intricate harmony of percussion instruments before finally coming to rest in the sink. He lowered his head and gripped the edge of the countertop with his strong hands, struggling to regain his equilibrium. "You drive me crazy", he mumbled, his low, rough voice nearly unrecognizable.

Olivia leaned against the kitchen island behind her. His back was turned, but if she reached out he'd be close enough to touch. His knuckles were turning white as his fingers dug into the gray countertop. His red t-shirt was stretched across his muscular back, emphasizing every deep breath he inhaled. Clearly, his body and mind were feuding; battling over what he should and should not do. She recognized the signs, because at that moment her body was waging a similar war.

"Strait jacket crazy or you-get-on-my-nerves crazy?" She asked curiously.

Grant chuckled softly, turning around to face her. He leaned his backside against the edge of the sink and reached for her. Hooking his finger in her belt loop he gave a firm tug, forcing her to move closer.

Suddenly her body was pressed against his. She could feel his powerful leg muscles against her thighs, could feel the swell of his sex against her belly. Her hands gently roamed over the ripples of his defined torso; up the wall of his solid chest.

God she felt good pressed against him. Her body was trim and lean, although she had mouth-watering womanly curves. She was the epitome of the perfect woman and he wanted her.

God, did he want her.

"Neither", he replied. Lifting her chin, he inched his mouth closer. "You drive me good-crazy, although the strait jacket might come in handy."

Olivia raked her teeth against her bottom lip, stifling a groan from Grant. "Why's that?" she asked breathlessly.

Grant lightly brushed his lips against hers as he spoke. "Because I have a hard time keeping my hands to myself when I'm around you."

He could feel her smile against his mouth. Unable to contain the mounting ball of lust in the pit of his gut any longer, he pressed his lips against hers and felt a surge of electricity arc between them. Her lips parted, urging him to taste. His tongue surged into her mouth with determination, the taste of her sinfully sweet tongue intoxicating his body with a potent mixture of desire and euphoria.

Rising onto her toes, Olivia wrapped her arms around his neck, desperately clinging to his steady body as her world was spinning.

A rough groan escaped from the back of his throat—she'd practically climbed his body in order to get closer. Gripping her waist, he pushed away from the counter and without interrupting their mating mouths, he backed her up into the living room. When the back of her legs collided against the tan sofa, he cupped her firm, curvaceous ass with his strong, eager hands and lifted until her feet left the sturdy floor beneath her.

Suspended in the air, she anchored her legs around his waist as he pivoted. His body collapsed onto the cushions, evoking a surprised gasp from Olivia, followed by a soft giggle as she landed in his lap.

Grant tore his mouth away from her lips, exploring the soft fragrant skin along her throat. She whipped her head back, giving him better access; encouraging him to continue. She could feel his fingertips brush against her chest as he slowly unbuttoned her blouse. She couldn't piece together a coherent thought. Her brain was temporarily out of order; her focus solely on the sensation of his open-mouth kisses along her throat.

Once her blouse was open he leaned his head back against the sofa and gawked at her body through hooded eyes. "God, Livvy, you're so beautiful", he groaned as his thumb brushed against the cup of her black lace bra.

Something about the way he looked at her— like he wanted nothing more in life than to feast on her body—turned her on. And when his thumb grazed the delicate lace of her bra, sweeping across her sensitive nipple, she arched her body toward his touch. Her head fell back again, followed by a gasp, and then an, *"Oh my God"*, when he tugged on the lace and covered one of her nipples with his mouth.

Damn, she was so fucking hot! He'd never seen a woman so responsive. And that's when he began to wonder: if she was this responsive and turned-on with practically all of her clothes on, how would she be lying beneath him while he was buried inside her...?

Taking her nipple into his mouth, he sucked and then gently raked his teeth against the hard pebble as he withdrew.

Another loud gasp.

And then...

Her hips rocked gently, grinding her sex against the hot length of his rigid cock. Suddenly he felt like a teenager again, getting-off on the slightest touch. But he wasn't sixteen—he was thirty-three. Old enough to hold back, although the woman currently straddling his lap had tested his self-control on more than one occasion.

Flicking his tongue against her, he watched as her chest moved with every quick, shallow breath. And when his mouth eased away from her nipple again, he pursed his lips together and blew softly.

A soft needy moan escaped her lips as she ran her fingers through his light-brown hair.

"You like that?" he asked in a rough, gravelly tone.

"Yeah", she whispered.

She was drowning in a pool of lust. Desire slamming into her for the first time in over a year; rushing over her like a raging current, carrying her to a destination full of promised pleasure.

Placing one of his hands on her delectable backside, he wrapped his free arm around her back and in one swift motion, turned her.

Suddenly she was lying on her back, looking up as Grant reached over his shoulder and grabbed a fistful of his shirt. Pulling the material over his head, the weight of his bare-chested body enveloped her. His mouth came over hers with urgency, their tongues dancing to the seductive melody consisting of thudding heartbeats and heavy breaths.

After swallowing her soft, sensual whimpers, his lips migrated to her neck. Her fingernails combed over his back as he began slowly grinding his hips against her center, imitating what he so desperately wanted.

"Oh, god... *Grant...*"

She was breathless, repeatedly chanting his name just above a whisper. So far gone she could hardly bear it.

Hearing his name on her lips was a potent aphrodisiac. He ground the snug fly of his denim jeans against her slower. Harder. Stifling a sound from her lips that indicated she was lost in her pleasure. Tugging on the lace of her bra, he revealed her firm pink nipple again. He nibbled, sucked, and licked until her hips bucked against him.

She was close—near the point of no return.

Panting.

Whimpering his name.

Her body begging for release.

Suddenly his ears were ringing.

Fingernails dug into his back.

Ears ringing. Hearts racing.

More ringing...

Grant froze as soon as he realized the ringing was coming from his on-call phone. Burying his face in the crook of her neck, he groaned. "You've got to be fucking kidding me..."

Their bodies remained still except for the movement caused by the rapid rise and fall of their chests as they attempted to catch their breath. The phone rang again and as he lifted his body away from her, they locked eyes. "Stay right there—don't move. I'll be right back."

Olivia watched as he walked away and suddenly felt a pang of regret.

How had this happened?

Panic erupted from her core, engulfing her. She hadn't meant for things to get this far.

Run!

She had to get away. Rising from the couch, she quickly tiptoed to the entry and grabbed her purse. She could still hear his voice in the kitchen.

Hurry!

Without a backward glance, she opened the front door and stepped out into the wet, turbulent night. She held her blouse closed with one of her hands while she descended down the wood steps, refusing to take an extra minute away from her desperate escape in order to button it.

"Eye witnesses indicate there is smoke and flames visible on the south and west sides of the wood structure", the dispatcher declared.

Grant released a heavy sigh. He was hoping the call wasn't a serious one; a call that didn't require his attention. He'd gladly refuse the overtime for an opportunity to finish what he'd started with Olivia. But sadly, that just wasn't going to happen right now.

"Fire engine is already en route."

"Alright, I'm on my way", he affirmed.

After placing the on-call phone on the counter, he started toward the living room. "You're not going to believe this, but—"

The couch was empty.

"Livvy...? *Olivia*...?" he called out.

Silence.

Grant grabbed his shirt off the floor and quickly put it back on as he headed for the front door. He snatched his keys from the entry table and opened the door to find Olivia backing out of the driveway in a hurry.

Damn it, Womack! You scared her off!

He would've liked nothing more than to chase after her. Apologize for...

For what, exactly?

They were both consenting adults. There was no mistaking the raw desire he saw in her eyes. She wanted him just as much as he wanted her, but he was beginning to realize that she wasn't the type of girl accustomed to "wanting."

Racing down the steps, he leapt into his truck. He needed to concentrate on putting out a fire and ignore the internal blaze currently engulfing him.

Grant removed his gear and placed it inside the fire engine before walking back to his truck. The fire had completely engulfed Mr. Steiner's old '63 Ford Pickup and would have consumed the entire detached garage it was stored in if not for the heavy November rain.

He inserted his key and started the ignition. It

was after midnight and he wondered if Olivia was still awake. He couldn't get her out of his mind. Could still see her wriggle beneath him with pleasure. Could still hear the sound of her panting his name. She'd been so close—another ten seconds and he would have made her come...

It was obvious that he and Olivia were attracted to one another. And even more obvious that she was battling their overwhelming chemistry. She'd fled his home as though her survival depended on it.

But why?

Suddenly, he remembered the conversation he'd had with Randall the night of Ty's Halloween party.

"How well do you know her?"

"Olivia?" Randall asked. "We grew up together. She was a year younger than me, but she was still one of my closest friends. Would've given anything to be more than friends, though."

"Had a secret crush, did ya?"

"Me and half the town's teenage male population! But she didn't really date much back then..."

"Why not?"

"Partly because she was too busy causing a ruckus to be tied down in a relationship. And partly because every guy on the island knew her free-spirit couldn't be tamed..."

Grant came upon his street and instead of turning left to go home, he made a right. He wanted to see Olivia; talk to her; finish what they'd started earlier on his couch.

His truck rolled to a stop in front of her house. All lights were out. "Damn it", he mumbled under his breath.

Well, apparently their unfinished business was going to have to be postponed. He just prayed that when daylight fell, the sun's brilliant rays wouldn't emphasize her regret.

CHAPTER 8

After the timer sounded, Olivia removed the exposed film from the tabletop enlargement machine and submerged it into the developer liquid. It'd been a long time since she'd used this machine. In the last decade, digital cameras had taken over the industry. Photographers loved the instant gratification of knowing whether or not they'd captured the perfect shot—hell, she was one of them! But there was just something about enlarging your own black-and-white prints. It was sentimental. Gratifying.

When the timer sounded again, she lifted the film from the developer liquid and sloshed it around in the stop bath before finally submerging it in the large tub filled with fixer solution.

Time spent alone in the darkroom had always been therapeutic. Her demons rarely haunted her there...

No such luck today.

She was still reeling from her dinner the other night with Grant. So talented was his lips, his tongue, his hands. She'd replayed their time together on his couch over and over again. She'd let her guard down and had given in to his pleasurable touch...

Big mistake.

Because now she knew how amazing he could make her feel and her body ached, longing to experience it again.

You don't do casual sex.

Right. Exactly. Because if her last date taught her anything, it was that men looked at women like a means to an end. An opportunity to fill a physiological need and once that need had been filled, you were no longer any use to them.

But Grant isn't like other guys—he's different.

And ironically, *that* was part of the problem. He hadn't pressured her—she'd been a willing participant. She'd allowed herself to indulge in the sensation of his kisses, his touch. There was no telling how far it would've gone if they hadn't been interrupted. He'd left her lying on the couch to answer his on-call phone and what did she do? Panicked and fled.

She'd put herself in a vulnerable position and she hated feeling like that. Instead of facing him, she'd chosen to sneak away. And as if that weren't bad enough, she'd purposely dodged his multiple attempts to get in touch with her.

Heavens to Betsy—she needed to stop dwelling on the mistakes she'd made the other night and instead, focus on the future. She couldn't exactly avoid Grant forever; it was a small island. Hiding out in her darkroom for the next month or two wasn't a viable option. Eventually their paths would cross and she really needed to be ready for when that moment occurred.

Working in solitude underneath the subtle red glow of the safe light had always eased her weary mind. In fact, it was just about the only place she felt completely safe—the outside world failed to penetrate the concrete walls. But somehow Grant had managed to do just that.

She'd just finished hanging her last enlarged print to dry when she heard a faint knock. "Who is it?"

"It's me, Grant. Can I come in?"

Oh god, now what?

This was the last thing she needed: time alone with Grant in a small, dimly lit room...

It was partly her fault though. He'd made countless attempts to get in-touch with her over the last several days and she'd ignored every single one of them. She was scared—*terrified*—of him.

Well, not of him—just how he made her feel. She was afraid she was beginning to like him just a little too much. And that *really* frightened her.

This "thing" between them was supposed to remain *casual. Fun*... but there was nothing casual and fun about her inability to resist him.

"Olivia?" he called again.

"Yeah, sorry... Um, make sure the door's shut behind you and the light's off."

When he gave her the indication that he'd followed her directions, she unlocked the door and opened it.

"Hey stranger", he greeted.

"Hi." Suddenly intimidated by the amount of space he took up, she hurried to her work area and unplugged the enlargement machine. She did her best to keep her hands busy, afraid if she allowed them to idle, they'd begin wandering over his body.

"What are you doing?"

Some of the prints she'd developed earlier in the day were now dry. She carefully unpinned them and placed the photos on the counter. "Just enlarging some of the pictures I took on the beach the other day." She could feel him approach from behind; felt a shiver of awareness zip down her spine.

"Can I see?" he asked.

Olivia handed him the small stack that'd dried and then turned around to gage his reaction. "What do you think?"

Flipping through the pictures, he laughed. She'd secretly captured their playful dip into the frigid water. "You're very talented."

"Thank you."

"You know, I have a confession to make: Dexter sneaking up on you was no accident."

Crossing her arms, she looked into his eyes. "Really? So Dexter's also your wingman?"

"Yeah... I saw you down on the beach and..."

"And what, Grant?"

After placing the photos down, he took a step forward and braced his hands on either side of her on the counter. "I don't know." Removing one of his hands, he began playing with a strand of her hair. "I wanted to be with you. I just really like being with you..."

The safe light above cast the small work room in a soft, red glow. And although the room was dim, she could still see the intense hunger in his eyes. He wanted her and god knows she wanted him, too. The memory of his tantalizing touch was still etched in her mind. She felt a sudden sense of euphoria come over her, whether it was from inhaling the developer solution or their immeasurable physical chemistry, she didn't know.

Most likely the latter.

She was at a crossroads. She could send him away and deny her body the pleasure she knew he could evoke, or simply give-in and face the consequences later...

"Lock the door", she whispered.

Grant let go of her hair and walked several paces to the right, turning the lock. He reached for her and pulled her closer to him. His mouth hovered over her lips for a few long beats, gently grazing over the surface, teasing her with every soft caress.

Her lips tingled. And when she couldn't contain the sensation any longer, she rose onto her toes and took control of the kiss. Her tongue charged into his mouth, connecting with his, communicating in an unspoken language.

He hadn't come here for this. His mission had been to simply talk to her—find out why she was suddenly avoiding him. But he'd found a better use for his mouth. Kissing Olivia was like breathing—it was essential for his existence. He was treading rough water and her lips were like a flotation device—he was going to cling to them for his survival.

Backing her up against the counter adjacent to the door, he ran his hands down her back and cupped her firm, round bottom and lifted. He sat her on the countertop and settled his body between the V of her legs. Running his callused hands over her smooth thighs, he peered into her hooded eyes. "I want you more than I've ever wanted anything", he mumbled.

Olivia smiled. "Wow, I guess I have some really big shoes to fill."

Grant reached over his shoulder, grabbing a fistful of his shirt, and quickly removed it. And after he tossed it aside, he assisted Olivia with the removal of her cotton blouse and white satin demi-bra. Completely bare from the waist up, he couldn't peel his eyes away from her beautiful body. He lightly pinched one of her pebbled nipples between his thumb and index finger as he kissed her neck. Slowly trailing open-mouth kisses along her collarbone before finally targeting her perfectly round breasts.

She inhaled a quick breath the moment his mouth settled over her nipple, her body recalling the memory of the last time he'd kissed her there days earlier on his couch. Her mind and body were waging a war: her brain busy listing all of the reasons why this was a bad idea, while her body encouraged her to finish what they'd begun.

Her body won the internal combat.

Fisting her fingers in his hair, she held him in place. She didn't want to think anymore, she just wanted to experience it—to feel him.

His hands glided across her silky skin. He wanted to touch her—everywhere—all at once. Her fingers were tugging softly in his hair, her breaths were swift and shallow, and the taste of her skin threatened to send him to another dimension. Suddenly, it wasn't enough—he wanted to get closer, *deeper*.

His lips ascended to her collarbone as his hands migrated to the hem of her faded denim skirt. He nudged the material up several inches when he was abruptly interrupted.

Olivia gripped his wrists. "Wait", she interjected breathlessly.

"What's wrong?" he asked as his mouth continued its assault on her shoulder.

"Nothing. It's just... it's been a long time. I don't do this sort of thing often.

"When's the last time?"

Olivia hesitated for a moment as she relished the sensation of his lips against the crook of her neck. "Um... over a year."

Shocked, Grant pulled back and met her gaze. "Over a year?" he asked in disbelief.

Nodding her head, she went on, "And before that, I can't even remember the last time. Look, I know I tend to act aggressive at times. But that's all it is—*an act.*"

Touched by her willingness to share something so personal about herself, he suddenly felt a twinge of guilt. She didn't do "physical relationships" and that admission made him respect her all the more. She was so unlike any woman he'd ever met and the last thing he wanted to do was pressure her into something she wasn't quite ready for. "Do you wanna stop?"

The fact that he asked made her heart swell a bit. No man had ever reached this point and then asked how she felt; they'd just assumed she was on board. At that moment rationale receded, all doubts faded. The only thought that remained was Grant—right now—with her—*inside her.*

"No. I'm just a little nervous, I guess", she softly admitted.

Grant cupped her face, his eyes boring into hers. "Don't be nervous. We'll go slow. And I promise, I'll make it feel good."

Oh. My. God.

If the pre-game festivities were any indication of his ability to make good on his promise, there was no doubt that the main event would leave her very satisfied.

And truthfully, that's all she really needed. There was no denying their chemistry. They were both clearly attracted to one another. Maybe sleeping with Grant *was* a good idea—she'd get him out of her system and the overwhelming urge to feel his hands on her body would lessen.

At least she hoped it would.

"Lift up", he instructed.

She complied, lifting her bottom as he hooked his fingers underneath the sides of her silk panties. He slowly lowered them down her legs and then tossed them to the ground before stepping between the V of her legs again.

After bunching her denim skirt up around her waist, his eyes feasted on her flawless body. Her figure was indefectible: firm, toned, yet round—perfectly proportioned for his pleasure. This moment—this woman—would star in his fantasies long after they were through.

Unable to resist any longer, he opened his wallet and grabbed a condom. Unbuttoning his pants, he lowered them and then quickly sheathed himself.

His body was ready and to ensure she was as well, he reached between the V of her legs and found her wet, slick, and waiting.

She moaned at his touch, the sweetest sound he'd ever heard. Desperate to hear it again, he gently pressed the pad of his thumb against her most sensitive spot and began moving it in soft, lazy circles.

"Grant", she panted. *"Please..."*

With his thumb still stroking her, he began kissing her neck, savoring the sound of her pleads, her breaths. "Please *what...?"*

"Please don't torture me", she begged.

Gripping the back of her lower legs, he tugged her body closer so that she sat on the edge of the counter. And then remembering his promise, he *slowly* penetrated her warm, slick center with his throbbing length.

Olivia gasped as he carefully nudged into her, her eyes wide with shock.

"You okay?" When she nodded her head, he plunged deeper, but he still couldn't enter all the way. "Wrap your legs around my waist", he instructed. He plunged again, this time stifling the sweetest whimper of pleasure. He could feel her tense body starting to relax, finally giving in to bliss.

"Holy shit, you're tight—you feel so fucking good..."

Her skin was ablaze, devouring her in a fiery ecstasy. Sex had never felt this good before, this intense. She longed for release and then silently cursed herself, never wanting the sensation to end. How was it that this man knew her body so well? Knew how to draw her out of herself?

He wanted to occupy her body completely, but he was still unable to fully enter her in their current position. Not wanting to place her on the cold concrete floor, he scooped his hands underneath her voluptuously firm bottom, hoisting her into his arms. Pivoting toward the door, he pinned her body against it and in one swift motion, lunged his rigid cock into her slick, snug heat.

She cried out his name as he buried his thick shaft deep into the depths of her body, the feeling so foreign, so intense—*so damn amazing.*

"Does that feel good?" he asked, his voice dripping with arousal.

"Oh, god, yes."

The sounds escaping her lips were so erotic. Not the fake kind of ear-piercing screams women often executed. No, these were unmistakably real.

Moans.

Soft whimpers.

Labored breaths.

He could probably get-off on her sensual sounds without even touching her. *But touching her...*

Feeling her slippery warmth gripping him felt so damn incredible! And then, of course, watching her as she absorbed his body: her hair slightly tousled, eyes fluttering, lips parted, and her soft skin glowing red underneath the safe light above had him teetering on the edge. But he had to hold back. He wanted to last for her. Needed to feel her body constrict around him when she climaxed and he knew she was close.

"Please... don't stop", she pleaded breathlessly. She'd never felt like this before. Her entire body was hypersensitive. Alert. She felt as if she were a butterfly erupting from its cocoon, seeing the world through a different set of eyes, leaving behind the constraint that confined its freedom. It was like she was having an out-of-body experience, hovering above, observing the metamorphosis taking place. Never had she felt so exposed, yet simultaneously, so aroused.

Forcing the weight of his upper body against her, he removed one of his hands from her backside and reached in front where they were joined. Stroking the pad of his thumb leisurely over her clitoris, he continued pumping into her.

Her body was drawing tighter, tenser. She was close—*so close.* "*Grant, please... I...*"

"Let go, Livvy."

"*I... I can't!*"

"Yes, you can. Let go—*come for me...*"

He watched as her head thumped back against the door, the rapidly expanding shockwave so intense she could no longer hold it upright.

Her body erupted, exploding and imploding, pleasure rushing over her in a cataclysmic blast. A wave of pure orgasmic energy channeled a path through her body like a swift river of liquid lava.

At the first sign of her impending peak, he pounded into her with purpose and when she finally surrendered with his name on her lips, he let go, too. Her tight muscles contracted around him, milking his submerged length, emptying his core. He groaned, cursed aloud, and then buried his face in the crook of her neck. Spreading soft, gentle kisses along her satin skin, he listened as their breaths gradually returned to normal.

"Are you okay?" he asked softly.

"Yeah. You?"

Removing his lips from her neck, he leaned his head back and gazed at her beautiful face through hooded eyes. "I'm better than okay... damn it, Livvy, you feel *amazing...*"

Raking her teeth against her plump bottom lip, her mouth turned upward in a seductive smile. And then, as quickly as her sated grin surfaced, it faded.

Awareness and reality overwhelmed her.

She'd had the most mind-blowing sex of her entire life. *With Grant—her brother's best friend...*

Jesus, Joseph, and Mary, this wasn't good.

He could feel the tension growing with her every breath. His arms were still holding her up and were it not for that, he knew she'd probably attempt to run away from him.

"We should probably get dressed. Ty'll be home soon", she informed him.

Grant hesitated for a moment. He didn't want to let her go—not like this. She was trying her damnedest to appear calm on the outside, but he saw through her guise. Inwardly she was freaking out. He observed her for a moment longer, stupefied over her swift transformation. She didn't appear angry, sad, happy... the interesting thing was, she was completely devoid of *any* outward signs of emotion. She was retracting before his very eyes—shutting him out once again.

"Yeah", he sighed. Lifting her body, he removed his sex from her center and then loosened his grip on her backside.

Slowly, she slid down his body until her feet came into contact with the cool concrete floor. Squeezing past his large muscular frame, she righted her denim skirt and reached for the rest of her clothes. She kept her back turned, terrified of the bewildered look in his eyes. She just needed some time. Time to recover and regroup. Time to figure out what the hell she was doing here.

CHAPTER 9

Kendall sat in the corner booth of the Board-walk Diner, one hand under her chin to support the weight of her head, her free hand tapping a rapid rhythm with her fingernails against the table's surface. She glanced at her watch just as Olivia arrived and then observed as her best friend slowly toddled toward her, her gait cautious and guileful.

"Sorry I'm late", she announced as she carefully slid into the seat across from her. Olivia opened her menu, skimming over the lunch specials when she suddenly sensed that Kendall was meticulously analyzing her.

"What?"

"Oh, nothing. Just making an observation."

"About...?" Olivia questioned.

Kendall took a small sip of her sweet tea and then placed her glass back on the table. "Well, for one, you're almost never late. You finally arrive, waddling in here like your nine months pregnant *and* to top it off, your skin's glowing a brilliant shade of satisfaction… If I didn't know better, I'd say someone got lucky."

"Shhh", Olivia gestured with her finger. "Do you mind keepin' it down?"

"So it's *true*", she whispered excitedly. You *did* get lucky!"

Olivia sighed. There was no point in denying it now. "Yeah, although I'm not feelin' so great about it right now."

"Why not?—"

"Alright ladies", the waitress interrupted, "what'll it be."

Kendall ordered a big, juicy bacon cheese-burger and onion rings. Olivia shook her head and smiled. She honestly didn't know where Kendall put it—the girl had the body of a model. Tall, thin: she could probably eat everything on the menu and still never gain an ounce. Olivia was in shape as well, although it didn't come naturally. She had to work hard to keep her figure, watching everything she ate and then running four or five days a week. She opted for a chef salad, dressing on the side.

When the waitress retreated, Olivia attempted to steer the conversation away from her sex-life. "So, how're things at the pharmacy?"

"Nice try. I'm not letting you leave here until you tell me everything about your little rendezvous with a certain fireman."

Damn, she should've known better. No way was a change in subject going to deter her best friend. "Alright, what do you want to know?"

"Um, *everything!*—where, when, how…"

Olivia cleared her throat. "Okay: in my dark-room, yesterday, up against the door."

Kendall's shoulders sank, her head cocked sideways, and her mouth dropped open. "Oh, c'mon, Liv—this isn't the game *Clue*. You know I need more details than that! Like: how'd he look?—is he big?—was it good? You know, details like that!"

Warmth spread across her cheeks as she recalled the vivid memory. It'd been a long time since she'd blushed this vibrantly. "Well, he's built like a Greek God—*a very well-endowed Greek God*—and he was absolutely *phenomenal*."

"Okay—so then what's the problem?"

"Besides the fact that he's Ty's best friend? He's... well, he's..."

Kendall crossed her arms and narrowed her gaze. "Oh. My. Goodness."

"What?"

"You like him—you *really like him!*"

Nervously she tucked a strand of hair behind one of her ears. "Don't be ridiculous! We're *just* friends. I'll admit I had a lapse in judgment yesterday, but it won't happen again—*it can't.*"

"Are you sticking to that story? Because do you want to know what I think?" Kendall asked, clearly amused by Olivia's reluctance to admit her true feelings.

"No—but I'm sure you're gonna tell me anyway."

"I think Grant scares the crap out of you! He's good-looking, charismatic, and any fool with half a brain can see he's crazy about you."

The waitress arrived with their lunch. She placed their dishes on the table and then warned Kendall to be careful with hers; it was very hot. After setting their ticket on the table, the waitress wound her way back into the kitchen.

"Good-looking, charismatic, yes—but *crazy* about me? No offense, honey, but I think that one's a stretch!"

"Now, see, that's where you're wrong!" Kendall said as she pointed one of her onion rings at Olivia. "No woman has ever kept his attention for longer than a week or two and none of those women have ever stepped foot into his beach house. You've managed to do both of those things. I could give you more examples if you'd like."

"No—that's okay. I get it."

Kendall popped the onion ring into her mouth and chewed. "So? Now what?" she asked curiously.

Olivia ran her fingers through her honey-blonde hair and sighed. "I don't know yet. I guess I just need some time to figure things out. Things were supposed to stay flirty and fun. Somehow I have to figure out how to get back to that..."

Hoping that her work would distract attention away from her "thing" with Grant, she entered the fire station in search of Chief Handler. She'd procrastinated long enough. A major newsworthy photo op wasn't going to fall into her lap, especially in this small island town.

Nope. If she wanted to catch a break, she was going to have to create her own favorable circumstances.

After knocking on his door, Chief Handler invited her to enter.

"Olivia! Nice to see you, honey", he said as he stood and came around to greet her on the other side of his desk. He enveloped her in a sentimental bear hug and then took a step back, settling his large derriere on the edge of his desk. "Ty's not on shift until Thursday."

"Yeah, I know. Actually I came here to see you."

"Well, alright then, have a seat", he said as he gestured toward the empty chair in front of him.

Olivia lowered herself onto the folding chair and winced slightly when her bottom came into contact with the cold hard metal seat. She needed to do this quickly and then head home to ice her very sore private area.

"What can I do for you?"

"Well, I'm sure Ty's mentioned that I'm a free-lance photographer."

"A time or two", he uttered as he winked at her. "He's very proud of you, you know—we all are!"

"Thanks Chief, I appreciate that! You see, my specialty is capturing pictures during times of tragedy and devastation: acts of nature and sometimes evil only mankind can cause. Anyhow, I've taken a hiatus from my usual routine of travelin'. And since Butler Island isn't the kind of place someone in my profession is likely to flock to, I was hopin' I could ride along with the department."

Chief Handler studied her for a few long beats, steadily chewing on his toothpick. "You want to take pictures while we're responding to calls?"

"Yes sir, I'd like to. Look, I know for the most part it's pretty slow around here. But I also know the town's seen its fair share of unexplained fires the last few months. One fire is probably accidental, two is coincidental; *five* fires in less than three months is darn-right suspicious!"

Chief crossed his arms over his large round belly. "So you think we have an arsonist on our hands?"

"Well, it's certainly a possibility, don't ya think?"

Without answering, Chief Handler stood from his desk and walked to his chair on the other side. After taking a seat, he reached into his bottom drawer, grabbed an extra on-call phone and then sat it on his desk. "Here are the conditions... One: you have to stay in the background. I won't risk your safety in order for you to get a good shot. Are we clear on that?"

"Yes sir—crystal."

"Good. Two: after you leave here, you'll need to head to city hall and fill-out the necessary paperwork relieving the department from any and all liability." When Olivia nodded her head in agreement, he went on. "Three: The city won't allow citizens to ride along during calls, so you'll have to provide your own transportation."

"That's not a problem, Chief—"

"—And last but certainly not least, any and all information you may hear is to be kept confidential. You're right—we have an arsonist at large and the worst part is we have no leads. The longer we can keep the residents on the island clueless about what we know, the better our chances of finding those responsible."

"You have my word, Chief. Thank you", she proclaimed as she rose from her chair. She gave the Chief a kiss on the cheek, grabbed the on-call phone from his desk and then headed out the door.

Next stop: city hall.

And then, an ice bath...

CHAPTER 10

Thanksgiving at the fire station hadn't changed since Olivia was a little girl. The entire department and their families gathered together every year to celebrate the holiday, each family bringing a dish for the pot luck luncheon, while the department supplied the main course. With the fire engine parked in the drive, the bay was free to house the festivities.

Rows of long tables and chairs were positioned to accommodate the crowd, but Olivia wasn't planning on sitting much. Not only were her girl parts still sore from her encounter with Grant, making long periods of sitting uncomfortable, the Chief requested she take pictures of the annual event as well.

Hard to capture the interplay and ambiance when her ass was glued to a folding metal chair...

Awareness assaulted Grant the moment Olivia arrived. It'd been four days since he'd spoken to her. Four days since he'd pinned her up against the door of her darkroom, naked. He'd known from the moment he'd left her that day what would happen. He was beginning to recognize a pattern: one step forward and two steps back.

Every time they reached a new milestone in their relationship, she withdrew. She'd disappear for a few days, ignoring his calls, avoiding contact at all costs. She was a control freak and she wasn't used to losing her grasp on it. He got it—he really did.

This whole "relationship" thing was new to him, too. He was deep in uncharted water and truthfully, he was a bit apprehensive about the course ahead as well. But there was just something about Olivia that he couldn't resist. It wasn't just her body—*lord knows he couldn't resist that.*

No, it was more than that.

He saw the beauty within her. The way she spoke straightforwardly, cared so deeply, loved her family and friends unconditionally.

She kept him on his toes and left him begging for more. He wasn't sure where their road might lead, but for the first time in his adult life, he was eager to find out. Eager to let go of the reins. Eager to let destiny run its course.

Not wanting to ambush her, he waited patiently as she mingled through the crowd, taking pictures and talking. He kept a watchful eye on her, trying to appear as nonchalant as possible, waiting for the perfect moment to make his approach.

It hadn't escaped her: Grant was monitoring her every move. No one else in the room seemed to notice, but she certainly did. Every time his eyes landed on her she felt a jolt of sexual energy. How he managed to do that to her when he was standing on the opposite side of the bay garage, she didn't have a clue.

She liked Grant.

There.

She said it.

Whatever *was* happening between them, it was more than simple friendship. More than a quick roll in the sack—or against a door.

And wasn't that the core of her dilemma? Grant was the kind of man she could easily fall for. And he was also the kind of man that could shatter her heart into a million little pieces...

She couldn't allow that to happen. She refused to mourn the loss of another person she cared about. Her heart told her to keep herself guarded—to protect herself at all costs.

Olivia felt two taps on her shoulder and then turned around.

"Hey, Olivia."

"Oh, hey, Jarrod. How're you?"

"Much better now", he said as he revealed a heartfelt smile.

Olivia returned the gesture. "Well, aren't you a perfect gentleman."

"I'll take that—I've been called far worse."

Crossing her arms, she tilted her head. "Somehow I find that hard to believe."

"Yeah, well, thanks..."

Jarrod shoved his hands in his pockets and rocked back on his heels. "So, um, I was wondering if a certain, beautiful, photographer would be interested in joining this gentleman for a drink later?"

"What, you mean one of those raw egg cocktails you're famous for?" she asked with a wide grin.

"No, I was thinking along the lines of something stronger. What do you say...?"

Dinner was essentially over. There were a few stragglers surrounding the buffet table for dessert and second helpings, but mostly the crowd mingled. Seeing an opportunity to catch a moment with Olivia, Grant started across the bay.

Along the way he was snagged by Chief Handler's wife, Debbie. He tried to make a quick getaway, but he should've known better. Debbie Handler was an extremely kind woman with a heart of gold, but boy did she like to talk. It didn't matter what about: weather, coupons, hell—the last time he'd been cornered, she'd divulged that cheese made Chief constipated. And when they'd attended a wine and cheese gathering at the Mitchell's residence earlier in the year, he'd consumed a month's worth of cheese in one night. She went on to describe how he'd been backed up for over a week and even went into detail about the various remedies he'd tried to get things moving again.

They exchanged greetings and before he knew it, she was telling him a story about the trouble she'd gone through yesterday when she'd cleaned the lint from the dryer.

"I stuck my hand in as far as it would go, but then I was terrified I'd get it stuck. And wouldn't that have been an interesting call? I can picture you boys sitting here at the station, moments away from eating your lunch, when suddenly dispatch interrupts with an emergency: 'We have an entrapment at 102 Second Street.' That's all I need—the jaws-of-life cutting me loose from my dryer. I mean, can you imagine?"

Fuck!

"I do have to say, though, my hands were laundry fresh by the time I was done! They smelled like I'd been outside picking wildflowers..."

Grant looked around—he desperately needed a way out of this conversation.

"...I recently switched dryer sheets. I used to always buy the fresh linen scent, but I have to tell you—that wildflower fragrance is so much better! I think it lasts longer on the clothes, too..."

He smiled a polite smile and ran his fingers through his hair. When he glanced back at Olivia, she was talking to Jarrod. She was smiling at him and Grant thought Jarrod was standing a little too close to her, the look in his eyes a little too lustful.

An overwhelming need to protect her washed over him. Jarrod was a good guy, but he clearly didn't have good intentions when it came to the beautiful blonde standing in front of him.

Admit it, Womack. You're jealous.

Okay. Yeah. So what if he was? Was that a crime?

"...I never understood why folks buy the liquid fabric softener. Most of the fragrance gets carried away in the rinse cycle. It makes more sense to use the dryer sheets. They perfume the clothes and help to ward off wrinkles—"

It's now or never.

"I couldn't agree more. Listen, can you excuse me for just a moment?" he asked as he patted her shoulder.

"Sure."

Grant moved around Chatty Debbie and pointed his work boots toward Olivia.

"I appreciate the offer, I really do, but truthfully I'm beat!"

Jarrod smiled and then studied the ground for a moment before meeting her gaze again. "Maybe some other time then?"

"Yeah, maybe..."

"—Hey, Olivia, can I talk to you for a minute?" Grant asked as he approached.

Raising her camera, she shook her head. "I'm sorry; now's not a good time. Ty's about to start the fire engine and turn on the lights and sirens for the kids. I don't want to miss a good photo op", She reiterated. Reaching for his forearm, she gave it a reassuring squeeze. "I'll catch up with you later."

"Yeah, okay..."

Grant watched as she walked away. What the hell did he expect? No way was she going to talk to him about what'd happened the other day in her darkroom *here.* Nope, he needed a new strategy and he suddenly knew exactly how to implement it. He'd let her walk away... for now. But something deep in his gut told him he couldn't let her walk away for good.

They were good together: mentally, emotionally, *physically.* In less than two months, this amazing woman had managed to wriggle her way into his heart. She'd managed to reach into the depths of his soul. A place he'd kept hidden for thirty-three years.

He was going to fight for her. Eradicate her

protective walls and puncture her ego until he uncovered the hidden treasure beneath. Because this rare beauty was a unique find, and damn it, he wasn't about to let the best thing that'd ever happened to him walk away.

Kicking off her shoes, Olivia left her bedroom and shuffled to the kitchen. It'd been a long, stressful day and with Ty still at the station until morning, she had the entire evening to unwind in private. She liked being home, sleeping in her childhood bed, but having lived on her own for the past nine years, she also enjoyed quiet time by herself.

Her plan: open a bottle of wine, sit in front of the fire pit on the patio, and try not to dwell on the mess she'd created with her personal life.

Easier said than done.

After an entire afternoon of restraint, Grant had finally approached her—no doubt wanting an explanation.

And he deserved one. But somehow when it came time to leave, she hadn't been able to find the courage or the words to explain her behavior.

This was just who she was. She didn't know how to be any other way. Losing control made her feel vulnerable. And she *hated* that—hated the overwhelming fear that enveloped her. Why couldn't she be like everyone else? Why did she always have to be in the driver's seat?

She embraced spontaneity when it involved her career—hell, being spontaneous as a teen landed her the nickname "daredevil." But when it came to personal relationships, she was *petrified.*

She wanted to continue to see Grant, but only on *her terms*...

So much for spontaneity.

Yeah. She was well aware of the irony. Her career as a freelance photographer sometimes led her to dangerous situations. She never thought twice about putting herself in harm's way in order to capture the perfect picture. The risks she took were almost second nature to her. Somehow, the thought of risking her heart—*her soul*—left her unprotected, defenseless, and susceptible to heartbreak again. She'd had enough heartbreak. She wouldn't endure it—couldn't—endure it again.

Olivia removed the cork from the bottle opener and reached above her for a wine glass when she heard the doorbell ring. She paused for a moment, knowing already who stood on the other side of the front door...

Grant.

Glancing at the clock on the stove she realized his shift had just ended five minutes earlier, which meant he'd immediately rushed here.

Setting her glass on the counter, she hurried to the front door to open it. "Hey, Grant."

"Mind if I come in?"

"Sure." Making her way back to the kitchen, she nervously tucked her hair behind one of her ears as he followed. "I just opened a bottle of wine. Would you like a glass?"

"Yeah, that'd be great."

Grant leaned his forearms against the bar and watched as she reached overhead into the cupboard for a second glass.

"Are you expecting company?" he asked as he

gestured toward the packaged fire log sitting on the counter beside her.

After taking a quick glimpse of the fire log, she met his curious gaze. "No. Why do you ask?"

Grant shrugged his shoulders. "Just seems like a lot of trouble to go through."

You fucking idiot—why did you say that?

"What—*this thing*?" she asked as she lifted it from the counter. "It doesn't get any easier than this, sugar. All I have to do is place it in the fire pit, strike a match, and enjoy."

"That's not what I meant... forget it—it doesn't matter."

"Okaaay", she responded cautiously. "Here", she said as she tossed the paper-wrapped log in his direction. After he caught it, she picked up both glasses of wine and started toward the French doors. "Make yourself useful. Matches are in the drawer beside the stove."

"I thought you said this was easy", he called out.

Olivia stopped and glanced over her shoulder. "Oh, it is. But why do it when I have a fireman at my disposal?" After revealing one of her gorgeous, gut-twisting smiles, she winked and then wandered onto the patio.

Grant chuckled softly under his breath—his feisty lil' Livvy was back.

Once he grabbed the matches from the miscellaneous drawer, he joined her on the patio, starting the fire with ease. Olivia had already hauled a lounge chair toward the fire pit and instead of dragging another seat close to the fire, he opted to sit with her. He wanted to be close to her—*needed to be close to her.* He lifted her legs and sat at the foot of the lounge chair, placing her lower legs back in his lap.

Silence enveloped them for a time—not an awkward silence—just a peaceful pause in conversation as their senses were riveted by the flickering flame. Its radiance hypnotized their eyes, the crackling melody echoing their contentment.

Taking a sip of wine, Grant broke the silence. "I'm sorry about earlier", he offered.

"Sorry? For what?" She asked confusedly.

"I saw you talking to Jarrod at the station and... I don't know... seeing the wine and the fire log, I just figured—"

"You were *jealous?*" she asked in disbelief.

Feeling a little uncomfortable with that label, he took another sip of wine and then clenched his jaw. Her adjective was accurate, but that didn't mean he liked it. "Um, yeah. Maybe a little."

"Jarrod asked me to have a drink with him, but I turned him down. I had a really stressful day; a crackling fire, wine... it seemed like a good way to unwind."

Keeping his eyes on the flames, he nodded in agreement. "That it is."

He paused for a moment, deciphering how he should proceed. He didn't want her to get defensive and recoil—not when things finally seemed like they were somewhat "normal" again. "So how've you been?"

"I've been great", she lied.

"No, you haven't—you can't fool me, Livvy... Why are you avoiding me?"

Removing her legs from his lap, she drew them in closer until her heels were flush against her rear end. "I didn't mean to avoid you. It's just... it—"

"—got a little too intense the other day, huh?"

Olivia cleared her throat and nervously tucked a strand of hair behind one of her ears. Talking about her feelings wasn't something she felt entirely comfortable with. "Yeah, something like that..."

Placing one of his hands on her knee, his thumb began caressing her skin, tracing imaginary circles along her knee cap. "Are you still sore?" he asked in a concerned tone.

"Why, are you ready for round two?"

"Baby, I was ready for round two five minutes after the first round ended. But I was pretty sure you weren't up for that."

"I was a little—sore—but it's getting better..." Olivia took a deep breath and sighed. She didn't want to hurt him, but she needed for him to understand her terms.

"Look, Grant, I know this is going to come out sounding like a cliché, but it's not you—*it's me.*" She observed as he scratched the light stubble along his jaw, noticing how tightly it was clenched. "The sex was great—*amazing.* The emotional part is..."

"Scary, I get it. Look", he said as he lifted her chin with his fingertips, "I like you and I really like spending time with you."

"Me, too", she whispered.

"Okay, now that we have that settled... I have an idea." Settling his body next to her on the narrow lawn chair, he cupped the back of her neck, running the pad of his thumb back and forth along her cheek.

"I'm listening..."

"From now on, *you* set the pace you're comfortable with. We can take this thing between us as fast or as slow as you want—just don't shut me out anymore. Okay with you?"

"Yeah, that sounds great." Olivia turned her body away from him, nestling her backside against the front of his body so that she faced the crackling fire. She thought about his offer. She'd never met anyone like him; what man would willingly want to be a part of this arrangement? She'd basically told him that their mind-blowing sexual encounter wasn't likely to happen again any time in the near future. And instead of abandoning her, *he stayed*.

Olivia bit back a moan as Grant ran his fingers through her hair. Resisting Grant was going to be harder than she first thought.

"Grant?"

"Yes?"

"Are you sure you're comfortable with a PG-13-type relationship?"

"If that's what you want, then, yes. I'll take whatever you're willing to give."

With his hands still gently combing through her hair, she was beginning to wonder: Could *she* handle a PG-13-type relationship with this incredibly appealing man?

Was that what she really wanted?

CHAPTER 11

"Hello?"

"Well, well, well—I was beginning to wonder if you were avoiding me. Missed you at the track on Saturday."

"Ah, yeah, um—sorry about that. I had to work."

"I understand. You have to make money, right? Money to pay your rent, put food on the table. *Pay your bills...*"

"Yeah, exactly." He heard a low, evil laugh erupt from the other end of the line, the eerie sound assuring him that his excuse wasn't amusing.

"I can relate. You see, I have to provide for my family as well. And that's hard to do when I'm not paid on time."

"I'm real sorry about that—I can have your money by this weekend."

There was a long pause before his bookie spoke again. "Let me ask you a question, son. Do you think I'm a reasonable man?"

"Yes. Yes I do", he nervously replied.

"Well, you're partly right. Usually I'm pretty easy-going—*except when it comes to little fuck-up's like you!*"

"Again, I'm real sorry. I'm gonna get some overtime this week and I get paid on Friday. I can have my payment plus ten percent", he offered.

"Make that twenty percent and not a penny less. Trust me, son, you don't want to fuck around with me. Bad things happen to good people when I'm not paid on time. Consider this your only warning; next time you won't receive a courtesy call..."

Grant hurried to the door and opened it.

"Miss me much?" Olivia asked with a dainty smile.

Reaching for her, he tugged her inside and slammed the door behind her. Unable to curb his appetite for the beautiful creature standing before him, he covered her mouth with his, devouring her with hungry kisses. Finally coming up for air, he pressed his forehead against hers and smiled. "A little."

"A little, huh? Well, I'd hate to see what would happen if you missed me a lot." Dexter sprung into action, doing his best to squeeze between them, his rapidly swaying tail slapping against her thigh with a loud, rhythmic thud. "I think somebody's jealous", she whispered.

"Looks like it."

Pulling away from Grant's strong, masculine arms, Olivia knelt down and began scratching the K-9's milk chocolate coat below his ears. "Did you miss me, too, boy? Huh...? Give me some sugar."

Eager to please, Dexter repeatedly lapped his tongue along her cheek and then abruptly stopped when Grant gave him the command to lie down.

"I hope you're hungry", he said as he led her into the kitchen.

"I'm starvin'!"

After dinner, they settled on the back patio, sharing a lounge chair and a blanket, listening to the steady pulse of waves washing ashore.

"It's so gorgeous out here tonight—not a cloud in the sky..."

"Oh yeah?" Grant briefly turned his attention away from her and looked above them. Thousands of stars glimmered against the ebony sky, a sight he'd gladly absorb if not for the rare beauty lying beside him.

Pinning her with his gaze again, he whispered, "I guess I hadn't noticed."

"I think someone's losing their perceptiveness."

Snuggling closer, he cupped the back of her neck. "Trust me—I'm well aware of my surroundings."

"Really?" she countered.

"Uh-huh. Like the way you bite your bottom lip when your thinking about something important, or the way your eyes turn a deeper shade of green when you're aroused. The way your lips feel when I kiss you—like a soft, satin pillow."

Closing the distance between them, he briefly pressed his lips against hers before spreading soft, sensual kisses along her jaw. "And that little sigh you release when I kiss you right here, below your ear."

The predictable sigh escaped her lips as his mouth kissed, licked and nibbled on her neck. It'd been almost two weeks since they'd agreed she would set the pace of their relationship. She was insistent on keeping their aura lighthearted and fun—*adamant about her clothes staying on*—but every time his lips touched her body, she longed to give in. Her body grieved, recalling the memory of him inside her, craving the sensual connection they'd shared in her darkroom.

Stay strong. You're not ready for the mound of emotions that would assault you afterward.

No—not even close.

She didn't want to deprive herself of the impassioned release he stimulated, but she also didn't want to hurt him. They'd have another earth-shattering sexual encounter, yes, but she knew herself. When they were through, she'd only push him away and she didn't want that.

She had to remain in control.

His hands maneuvered over her body, his fingers aching to get under her clothes.

Damn, he wanted her.

Wanted to spend the rest of the night exploring every inch of her beautiful body with his eyes, his hands, *his mouth.* With every passing minute it became exponentially more difficult to resist her.

God, how he wished things were different. He'd gladly give his right arm if he thought it would chase her fear and insecurities away. Since that clearly wasn't an option, he'd have to settle for patience. Because with time, he knew she'd begin to trust him. And when she did...

His senses were on alert: he heard the crescendo

of her breaths; recognized the desire behind her hooded eyes; inhaled the intoxicating vanilla scent on her body; relished the sensation of his lips grazing against her silk-like skin. *And her taste...*

"God, your skin tastes so good", he mumbled as he swept open-mouth kisses along the base of her throat. "It makes me wonder..."

Closing her eyes, she suppressed a fleeing whimper. "About...?"

Voice dripping with arousal, he replied, "If you taste this delicious everywhere."

Oh. My. God.

Before she could respond—*before she could weigh the pros and cons of exploring third base*—their on-call phones rang.

Their bodies froze.

"Déjà vu", she uttered.

"Damn it... yeah", he said as he reluctantly stood up and offered his hand. "C'mon, you can ride with me."

Olivia allowed him to assist her to her feet and then shook her head. "That's probably not such a good idea. Having to explain how we ended up together tonight is not something I feel like gettin' into. And you know how everyone in this town is—we show up together and the next thing you know, we're *dating*."

Clearly amused, he smiled. "Well, we are; aren't we?"

"Maybe... but no one needs to know that—*especially Ty.*"

"Good point", he agreed.

* * * * *

Billows of smoke erupted from the rooftop of the small theater, obscuring the dark, naked sky; liberating itself from the blaze below. Flames licked at the roof and front entry, the heat so intense, Olivia feared she'd singe her eyebrows if she stood closer.

Upon arrival, Ty and Randall had already fastened the hose to the nearby fire hydrant. Water spewed from the opening, drenching the apex of the abandoned brick building with a liquid antidote. Chief Handler was busy calling out orders for Grant, Jimmy, Mark, and Jarrod to carefully access the building from the rear, where there didn't appear to be any visible flames at the moment.

The theater had closed its doors over the summer. The owner of the one room auditorium was no longer capable of sustaining profits with the economy in shambles. The islanders' needed to spend their extra cash on groceries for their families; fuel to transport them to and from work—not on a second-run movie, a large popcorn, and a thirty-two ounce Coca Cola.

Most likely the building was empty, but Chief wanted them to make a quick sweep of the interior to ensure there weren't any potential victims inside.

"I want you in and out in a jiffy, you hear?" he instructed.

Unable to be heard through their masks and breathing apparatuses, the four brave firemen nodded and then turned to enter through the rear door.

The risks firemen took never ceased to amaze her. It took a special breed of man to willingly step into a raging incinerator, venturing into a structure that rivaled a hot, flaming hell for the sole purpose of saving lives.

Crouching low, Grant and the other three men quickly meandered through the auditorium. They'd already searched backstage and a small portion of the theater when Grant gave the signal to retreat. The lobby was completely engulfed and the searing flames had already begun devouring much of the seats in front of them.

Over the roar of the flames, he heard a sound that would terrify the bravest of firemen. It began as a subtle creak and then transformed into a loud, angry moan.

"Womack, get outta there!" he heard Chief Handler yell over the radio.

Leaping onto the stage, Grant shouted through his mask at the three men beside him. "Roof's about to collapse! Get the hell out!" Pushing the men in front of him, he followed behind.

Olivia waited toward the rear entrance, making sure to keep a safe distance. She'd already captured hundreds of pictures since her arrival and once she'd heard the Chief give the order for Grant and the other men to exit the building, she'd placed her camera on the tripod and activated the time-lapse feature. No way could she keep a steady hand or concentrate when four people she cared about were surging toward safety.

FLASH.

The thundering sound of the weakened roof collapsing near the front of the building enveloped her in a paralyzing panic. In her peripheral vision, she could see the flash of her camera flicker in five second intervals, but somehow time seemed to proceed in slow motion.

FLASH.

She could see the look of uncertainty in Chief Handler's expression as he shouted into his radio for them to run, but the sound was muffled by her labored breaths and raging pulse.

FLASH.

The earth vibrated under her feet as the large wood beams fell to the ground. She covered her mouth in horror.

FLASH.

Suddenly, a silhouette burst through the murky black smoke, followed by three more. Olivia let go of a breath she hadn't been aware she was holding as the men raced toward her.

FLASH.

The last man to exit the inferno removed his hat and breathing mask...

Grant.

FLASH.

His bright white smile contrasted vividly against the black soot around the edges of his face. Instead of her heart rate returning to normal, it seemed to skip a beat and then rapidly flutter. Olivia rubbed her breastbone with the heel of her hand, overwhelmed by the flood of emotions assaulting her. She'd been terrified for the four men and was relieved that they'd all made it out safely.

But it was more than that.

The thought of anything happening to Grant made her weak in the knees—*weak in the heart.* Because suddenly it became quite clear that he was beginning to mean more to her than a fun flirty fling and as scary as that admission was, she embraced it.

CHAPTER 12

Winterfest was a longtime tradition of Butler Island. It was a community celebration, held the first weekend in December, signifying the beginning of the holiday season. The festivities began with the Christmas parade down First Street, followed by the annual Christmas cookie bake-off, and finally ended with the carnival.

Ty took her every year growing up and this year was no exception. They began their afternoon together as spectators for the parade. It hadn't changed much in the last ten years: she recognized some of the same floats, same costumes—even the convertible Miss Winterfest rode in was the same.

Gesturing toward the blue convertible, Ty said, "I remember when you were Miss Winterfest. Gosh, it seems like just yesterday..."

"I know. Weird, isn't it? Nine years..."

Ty nodded. "I came every year; it just wasn't the same without you."

"You're not gonna get all mushy and sentimental on me, are you?"

Chuckling, he replied, "Nah, I know better!"

After the parade they wound their way through the booths positioned along the boardwalk. They sampled dozens of Christmas cookies for the annual bake-off and when their veins were surging with adrenaline and excess sugar, they trekked toward the carnival.

The horizon teetered on the edge of darkness as they climbed aboard the Himalaya. The ride was a childhood favorite—she loved the blaring music, the dancing lights, the swift acceleration. The lap bar came down and after the ride attendant personally checked that it was locked into position, he scurried to his controls.

The distinct sound of a lone guitar, followed by the heavy thud of a drum...

The ride accelerated with such force it threw her body against her brother as The Rolling Stones' *Paint It Black* blasted from the speakers. A rush of cold air collided against her face and laughter fled her lips as she raised her hands above her head.

Grant stood behind the metal barrier, mesmerized. Olivia appeared to be having the time of her life: her hands in the air, an unmistakable expression of content and bliss adorned to her beautiful face.

He wondered if she knew how spellbinding she was?—wondered if she suspected he was beginning to fall for her...

Probably best to keep that bit of information to yourself, Womack.

* * * * *

Olivia glanced at Ty as the ride came to a halt. "You okay?" she asked.

"Why do you ask?" he countered as he released his white-knuckled grip on the lap bar.

"Oh, I don't know. I guess because you're face is ten shades of green right now."

Ty felt his cheeks. "That obvious, huh? I guess I can't hang like I used to—I'm getting old!"

"C'mon, let's go get you a drink."

Grant observed as they exited the ride and advanced toward him. "Hey—*geez, bro,* you look like shit! You feel alright?" he asked Ty.

"Never better", he sarcastically remarked.

"Oh, look"—Olivia interrupted— "bumper cars!" She pointed directly across from where they all stood. "C'mon, Ty, let's ride real quick and then you can get a drink."

Rubbing his stomach, he shook his head. "No can do. I'm gonna have to sit this one out. You go ahead—Grant can go with you."

Olivia turned to look at Grant. She lifted an eyebrow, assessing her competition. "I don't know; I don't think he can handle me."

Grant crossed his arms over his broad chest and smirked. He could recognize a challenge brewing. "Oh, I think I can manage you just fine."

"Okay, care to make a friendly wager then?"

"Name your terms."

"Whoever crashes into the other first, wins; loser pays for the winner's cotton candy."

"You've got yourself a deal."

They left Ty sitting on a nearby bench and

then rushed toward the bumper cars. Patiently they waited as the current round ended.

Standing behind her, Grant leaned forward until his mouth was inches from her ear. "Don't worry", he whispered, "I'll take it easy on you."

Olivia glanced over her shoulder. "Take it easy on me? Sugar, you won't even be able to keep up, let alone take it easy on me."

"Is that right?"

"Most definitely..."

Moments later, they were ushered inside. Olivia sprinted toward the hot pink number seven car while Grant chose the green number two. With his body buckled and a firm grip on the steering wheel, he took a gander at Olivia. Gnawing on her bottom lip, she stared back with a bold determination in her eyes—clearly she had her "game face" on.

The buzzer rang, delivering the tiny vehicles the power to move. His eyes were transfixed on Olivia. She was on the opposite side of the arena, steadily—and quite aggressively—crashing into anyone within her vicinity. Over the screeching and the hammering clash of cars colliding, he could hear her laughter. God, she had the most infectious laugh— the kind that reverberated throughout his entire body. Hearing it made him smile.

BAM!

Olivia slammed into the side of Grant's green car at full speed.

His head thrashed like a whip. When he looked back, she was smiling like she'd won the lottery and then her delicate features took on a predator-like expression.

BAM!

So she'd won the bet—*that didn't mean she was going to take it easy on him*. She followed closely behind his car, determined to get in another good strike before the buzzer rang again.

The girl was persistent; he had to admit. He saw firsthand why so many of the people in town referred to her as "daredevil": her feminine and flawless exterior betrayed by her fearless and aggressive nature. The sight sent lust surging through his veins—which was quickly obliterated by a thundering crash as she smacked into him again.

The cars lost power as the buzzer rang. Grant shook his head in disbelief as he exited his car and advanced toward her. He offered his hand, assisting her out of her pink hot rod.

"Don't look so surprised, Womack", she said as she smiled.

"You cheated", he proclaimed.

"What? You can't *cheat* in bumper cars! That's the silliest thing I've ever heard!"

After exiting the ride, they headed toward Ty.

"Who won the bet?" Ty called out as they approached.

"Who do you think..."

Ty glanced at his best friend. "You let a *girl* beat you?"

"She's not just a *girl*—she's *daredevil*", he explained. "Besides, she cheated."

"There you go throwin' that word around again. Do you mind explaining how I *'cheated'* at bumper cars?" she asked as she crossed her arms.

"You were laughing so hard. It was... distracting."

"Nice try, Womack, but you still owe me a bag of cotton candy."

Grant raised his hands in surrender. "Alright, alright, I'm a man of my word. I'll be right back."

Olivia lowered herself on the bench beside Ty. "Can you believe him?" She asked in disbelief. "So, feeling better?"

Ty leaned forward, resting his forearms on his knees. "Worse. It probably wasn't the best idea to ride the Himalaya after I wolfed down about two-dozen Christmas cookies."

"Well, I'd have to agree with you on that one!"

"Listen, I'm thinking about heading home."

"Oh... alright—"

"You guys are leaving?" Grant asked as he returned with a large bag of Christmas-colored cotton candy.

"Think so—there's a bottle of Pepto-Bismol at home with my name all over it!" Ty informed him.

"Olivia, if you want to stick around for a while I can take you home later", Grant offered. They were just beginning to have fun—he wasn't quite ready to end the evening yet.

"That alright with you, Ty?" she asked.

Rising to his feet, he nodded and then slapped Grant on the shoulder. "Anything happens to her and I'll feed you my fist for breakfast. Are we clear?" he asked, half joking—half not.

"Crystal." Grant waited until Ty was out of earshot. "And then there were two..."

In no hurry, they decided to take a stroll. It was nice to be out in the open, not having to hide that they were spending time together. It was okay if someone happened to start a rumor that they'd spotted them together; Ty knew they were hanging out tonight—they just had to be careful with PDA (public displays of affection).

"Thanks again for the cotton candy."

"You're welcome."

"So, still think I cheated?" she inquired.

Grant revealed one of those bone-melting smiles he'd perfected over the years. "You don't play fair", he explained.

"Oh, that's right: you think I was purposely distractin' you."

"Damn straight—everything you do distracts me…"

Olivia turned to face him and pressed her bottom lip against her teeth. "Well, today's your lucky day", she said as she gestured toward the row of carnival games up ahead. "Feel like redeeming yourself?"

"You're on."

They landed at a game that required a good eye and a steady hand—two things he was sure he didn't possess simultaneously. Clutching a rifle, they were supposed to shoot rubber pellets at multiple moving targets. Each target was worth a set amount of points; the more you accumulated, the bigger the prize.

"So what do I get when I win?" she asked confidently.

"We can figure out the details later."

He watched as Olivia picked up the rifle and got into position.

"I hope you're ready to get your ass kicked again, Womack."

"Bring it on, darlin'."

He fully expected for her to randomly eject several rounds of rubber pellets without even coming close to any of the targets.

Wrong again.

As soon as the game attendant blew the whistle, Olivia fired her weapon like a sharp shooter. She aimed with the kind of precision that could only be carried off by someone who was comfortable handling a firearm. And when their sixty seconds of target practice was through, she'd won again.

"Remind me to never piss you off", Grant commented wryly.

Olivia turned and exposed a playful scowl.

"Alright, ma'am, what'll it be?" the attendant asked.

Olivia smiled and pointed to a stuffed teddy bear hanging behind him. "I think I'll take that bear behind you—the one that's dressed like an angel." The man picked up the bear and tossed it toward her. "Thanks."

Silence lurked between them as they started to walk away. Finally, Grant spoke. "My ego's a little bruised."

"Aw, poor baby."

"It's okay, you can make it up to me later", he suggested with a wry grin.

"Really? What exactly did you have in mind?"

Reaching for her hand, Grant slipped behind one of the game booths where they could have some privacy. Alone for the first time since they'd been interrupted by the theater fire, he pressed her up against the rear of the booth. "This", he whispered as he cupped her face. He aligned their mouths, but this kiss wasn't like all the others.

Although desire and need pulsed through his body, he remained in control. It was unhurried, attentive, tender. The kind of kiss a man only unleashed when he wanted to convey how deeply he cared.

"Sorry about that", he uttered as he pulled away. "I couldn't help myself."

Olivia lightly brushed her fingertips across her tingling lips before resting the palm of her hand against his solid chest. "It's okay. You were beat by a girl twice in one night; obviously I questioned your masculinity", she playfully explained.

Grant smiled in spite of himself. He loved her quick wit; it kept him on his toes. Most girls would've been clingy or downright boring by now.

But not her.

After they left the carnival they sat in the driveway in his truck, their mouths mating, their hands wandering. He'd never felt this way about anyone before. He wanted more than anything to take her back to his bed and spend the rest of the night making love to her.

But he couldn't.

He'd told her she had to set the pace and if she wasn't ready to take that leap with him, he certainly wasn't going to push. He was eager to hear her say she wanted him—*eager to watch her come again.*

Until then, he'd settle for this: making out like two love-crazed teenagers in the front seat of his truck.

Oh, how life was good...

CHAPTER 13

"What time did you get in last night?" Ty asked as he carried his bowl to the bar.

Olivia stood at the stove, carefully spooning her cheese grits into her bowl. "Um, just before midnight."

"Did you have a good time?"

"Yeah, it was fun", she uttered, trying to sound as nonchalant as possible.

There was a momentary pause, and then...

"Was Grant on his best behavior?"

Olivia froze and then quickly recovered by turning around, taking a seat at the bar. "*Yes*", she answered cautiously. "Why do you ask?"

Because I've seen the way he looks at you... "No reason—just wanted to make sure."

After the awkward conversation with Ty at breakfast, Olivia settled into her darkroom to check on her enlargements. Yesterday, before the Winterfest Parade, she'd enlarged some of the photographs taken the night of the theater fire and had left them to dry. Carefully, she unclipped the black and white prints and flipped through them.

She was impressed with how well they'd turned out. She'd captured Ty and Randall hosing down the front of the building; Chief Handler shouting orders in his handheld radio; various angles of the brick building consumed with hellish flames.

But her favorite was the one she'd captured of Grant.

It was taken automatically by her time-lapse feature as the roof was collapsing. He had just e-merged from the blaze and was running toward the camera. His hat and mask had already been removed and black soot was smeared around the edges of his face. Behind him was a thick haze of smothering smoke.

But that's not what made this picture her favorite.

There was something about his blue eyes— they were ironically translucent, revealing his mind, his heart. Relief that he and his "brothers" had made it out of the collapse unharmed.

And weakness.

Not for the punishment his body had just endured—but for *her*. A realization that for the first time in his life, he was running toward something— or someone—that mattered...

This was the kind of photograph that Adversity Magazine loved: an image that stimulated an emotional response. On Monday, she was going to head to the post office and send it off. Olivia smiled at the notion: who would've thought that her latest masterpiece would star her hometown?—*her hero*?

* * * * *

Olivia sighed as she positioned herself behind the wheel of her Mini Cooper. A familiar wave of gratification and content washed over her. Buckling her seatbelt, she turned the ignition and maneuvered her vehicle out of the post office parking lot. She felt this way every time one of her photographs was en route to its published destiny. Some people were addicted to drugs or alcohol; others gambling. But for her, an overwhelming sense of euphoria seeped from her pores whenever she satisfactorily submitted a meaningful and expressive work of art.

The late afternoon sun was steadily plummeting from the western sky, transforming the atmosphere into a canvas of variegated brilliance. Instead of heading home, she decided to use the picturesque ambiance to her advantage.

After she'd received permission from Chief Handler several weeks ago to accompany the fire department on their calls, she'd visited city hall. Chief had requested she fill-out the necessary paperwork relieving the department from liability in the event she was to become injured. Thankful for the opportunity she'd been given, she'd immediately traveled there.

During her brief visit, Mayor Cliffburg had propositioned her. He'd explained that the newly renovated building lacked artwork and asked if she'd be willing to provide her services. She'd accepted his offer, aware that opportunities to make money in the small town were few and far between. Olivia had concocted the idea of photographing various landmarks on the island and the mayor immediately fell in love with the concept.

So with sunset looming and her euphoric mood intact, she decided to head to the first landmark on her list: the boat warehouse. It had a vintage appearance; one that she thought would benefit from both color and black-and-white photography.

Located adjacent to the marina, the warehouse specialized in repair and maintenance of the area's numerous watercrafts: everything from Jet Ski's to fishing boats to sailing vessels. The warehouse was temporarily closed due to damage it incurred from the tropical storm that'd skirted along the Florida Panhandle back in early October, but the owner, Mr. Morgan, had given her special permission to photograph the interior and exterior of the metal building.

After parking her car near the marina, she cased the exterior, searching for the perfect angle that not only captured the enormous structure, but also showcased the kaleidoscopic sunset above. Once she was satisfied with the amount of images outside, she carefully entered the building.

Beams of light infiltrated the large windows near the ceiling, casting a radiant glow to portions of the dimly lit storage facility. Her eyes scanned the room in a smooth, panoramic motion, finally landing on a small sailing vessel located in the back corner. She quickly journeyed toward it, her camera emanating a rhythmic "click" as she accumulated images. Realizing that she had roughly twenty minutes of daylight left, she trekked along the back of the warehouse, when suddenly she discovered she wasn't alone.

She caught a glimpse of a man dressed in black, his face covered with a dark ski mask. He was meandering through the aisles toward the middle of the building, randomly dumping liquid on the boats surrounding him. Olivia hid behind a fourteen foot Pontoon boat parked along the back of the dim warehouse, relentlessly photographing the event.

And then, the unthinkable—

He struck a match...

In an instant, she heard a *whoosh*, witnessed a ball of fire, felt a rush of searing heat. She raised her arm, shielding her face from the intense blaze and when she removed it, the mystery man in black had disappeared.

She needed to get out of there.

Fast.

After fleeing the burning warehouse, Olivia reached into her pocket for her cell phone and called for help. Less than five minutes later, the fire engine arrived, along with several of the department's finest following closely behind in their personal vehicles.

Olivia observed Chief Handler directing the scene, carefully examining the blaze like a flame whisperer and then calling out orders to extinguish them.

"This is the work of an arsonist", she said as she approached.

Never removing his eyes from the flames, he answered, "Most likely. But we won't know that for sure until we extinguish the fire and search the building for evidence."

"There's no need, Chief. I was here when the fire started."

"*What?*" he asked as he turned to face her.

Olivia handed him her camera. "It *was* arson. Here's your proof."

* * * * *

"Alright, now that everyone's here, let's get started", Chief Handler announced as he stood in front of the enormous flat-screen T.V. in the corral of the fire station.

"I'm sure you're all wondering why I called a mandatory meeting this morning... As you are all aware, the island has seen an abundance of fires in the last several months. We've all speculated as to how these fires were started. At first, we believed it was purely coincidental. But as the numbers increased, our opinions rapidly changed."

"Investigations by the state fire marshal corroborated our theory, but we still had zero leads— *until now*. It appears as though we are dealing with a lone arsonist. And I can say this with confidence, because Olivia witnessed the arsonist in action."

"What was she doing there?" Jimmy asked.

"From what I understand, the mayor hired her to photograph various places around the island. Basically, she was at the wrong place at the right time."

"So did she get a good look at them?" Randall inquired.

"Not them—*him*. And unfortunately she wasn't able to make an ID; he was wearing a ski mask."

"So, Chief, if the arsonist was wearing a disguise, how can we be sure it was a 'he'?" Jarrod questioned.

"I asked that question, too. Olivia said, and I quote, 'if it wasn't a man, then the town is being burnt to the ground by Chyna Doll, the woman wrestler.'"

Everyone laughed. WWE had been a favorite source of entertainment for years and although the woman wrestler was retired, everyone was familiar with her appearance. How could they not be?—she had bigger biceps than half the guys at the department.

"Olivia may not have seen his face, but she still captured him setting fire to the warehouse on her camera. We're getting closer to catching this guy..."

Shit, they're on to me!

He tried to maintain his poker face; tried not to squirm like a bucket of earthworms in his seat. How could he have been so irresponsible? He knew better than to set a fire without searching the premises first.

He'd gotten careless—driven by the need for overtime money and fear of what his bookie would do to him if he was late on another payment.

Next time, he *would* be more careful.

But until then, he needed to destroy what little evidence they had on him and he knew exactly where to start...

Little Miss Olivia...

CHAPTER 14

With another shift successfully completed, Grant drove to Olivia's. It had become a part of their routine: every third day, he left the fire station and spent time with her. Keeping their relationship hidden was becoming more difficult by the day, but if sneaking around was the only way to make her feel comfortable, then he was more than willing to oblige.

After parking his truck along the street, he drifted toward the front door and rang the doorbell. Within moments Olivia answered the door, the sexy little number she wore rendering him almost speechless.

"What's the matter, Womack? Cat got your tongue?" she teased as she held the door open.

His eyes swept down the length of her body. Her honey-blonde hair was haphazardly clipped to the top of her head, random strands falling around the frame of her face. A jade terrycloth jacket covered much of her upper body, except for the fact that it was unzipped midway; exposing a navy tank top underneath. His eyes traveled further south, focusing on a matching jade mini skirt that made her killer legs appear longer than they actually were—and he should know; several weeks ago those seductive legs were wrapped around his waist. Finally, his gaze landed on her perfectly pedicured feet, her toenails painted a pale shade of pink.

"Grant, hello...?" she uttered as she waved her hand in front of his face. "Are you still with me?"

Realizing he'd been staring, salivating at the sight of her, he briefly shook his head, transporting his mind back to reality. "Yeah, I'm with you", he said as he wrapped his arms around her. "For much of the night..."

After his unexpected trance, they fell into their usual routine: dinner, wine, and great conversation. They'd been sitting on the couch for a while, recounting their day, when Grant finally divulged the specifics about the department's meeting earlier that morning.

"Chief mentioned you were there and caught the arsonist in action. Why didn't you say anything?" he asked.

"I didn't *want* to keep that bit of information from you, but Chief Handler made me swear not to tell anyone until he had an opportunity to speak with you guys."

Grant sighed as he gently nudged a stray lock of hair away from her left eye. "I'm so thankful the guy didn't see you—there's no telling how he would've reacted had he realized he wasn't alone."

Glancing down at her lap, she nodded. "I know. Luckily, I kept hidden; he never suspected I was there..."

"It was risky—*too risky!*"

"Speaking of '*risky situations*': Do you have any idea how close you came to that roof collapsing on you last week at the theater fire?"

"That's different—"

"How so?" she asked curiously.

Grant shrugged his shoulders. "It's my job... It's what I'm paid to do."

Olivia tucked her feet underneath her and began picking at her fingernails. Grant studied her for a few long beats. Something was bothering her and she appeared to be fighting an internal war over whether or not to share it with him. He tilted her chin up with his fingertips and met her gaze. "Talk to me. What's wrong?"

"You scared me—that night at the fire—you *really* scared me. When I heard the roof collapse, I thought—"

"Hey", he mumbled softly as he reached for her and pulled her onto his lap. "It's okay—I'm okay. I've been doing this for a long time; nothing bad's going to happen to me."

Olivia stared into the depths of his blue eyes and the next thing she knew, she was inching forward. She pressed her lips against his and when he parted his lips, her tongue surged into his mouth with an animal-like intensity.

A predator consuming its prey...

She was through with deprivation. She didn't want to starve her body any longer. She wanted to indulge—devour everything he was willing to give her—until she was thoroughly satiated.

Following her lead, he ravaged her with his kiss. He was teetering on the edge of control, clenching his hands to restrain himself. Letting go—free falling into a sexual abyss—wasn't an option. He wanted her—more than his next breath—but he needed to know that she wanted him, too.

Gripping her shoulders, he respectfully pushed her away and then gawked at her through hooded eyes. "I don't want you to start something that we can't finish", he mumbled in a gravelly voice he barely recognized. "I want you so damn bad it hurts, but I won't do this unless you tell me."

Biting her plump bottom lip, Olivia stood and offered her hand. When he accepted, she helped him to his feet and then turned, leading him down the hall to her bedroom. After turning on the small lamp adjacent to her antique white canopy bed, she pivoted to face him.

He stood in the doorway, his shoulder leaning against the doorjamb, perusing her body as she unzipped her jacket and shrugged it down her bare arms. Then, grasping the bottom edge of her navy tank, she raised her arms, removing the thin stretchy garment; revealing two perfectly round breasts.

"I want you", she whispered, her gaze never leaving his.

Grant expelled a puff of air from his lungs. It was hard to concentrate with Olivia standing in front of him, *topless*. "What about afterward? I don't want you to spend the next week avoiding me."

Slipping her thumbs underneath the waistband of her skirt, she nudged the material down her legs, along with her delicate lace panties. "That's not going to happen", she assured him. "I want to do this—*I want you…*"

Savoring her words, his eyes feasted on her

perfectly sculpted, bare body. He groaned when she reached up and removed the clip from her hair, captivated by the way the ends of her blonde locks settled around the curve of her breasts. His attention traveled south along the firm plane of her taut, yet feminine stomach, finally focusing on the thin, dark strip of hair that barely covered her mound.

Holy shit—she waxes!

His bulging sex pressed against the fly of his cargos at the discovery. The last time they'd been this intimate, they were in her darkroom. It was dimly lit; he could see enough of her body to know it was utterly flawless, but it'd been too dark to really *"see"* her.

Thank you, Thomas Edison, for inventing the light bulb. I'm forever indebted to you...

Olivia smiled as she cleared her throat, hoping to regain his undivided attention. "Well, are you gonna just stand there and stare at me?—or are you comin'?"

Pushing off the doorjamb, Grant reached over his shoulder and grabbed a fistful of his navy fire department T-shirt, yanking it over his head as he slowly walked toward her. "Oh, I'm coming", he assured her, his voice laced with lust. Finally standing in front of her, he tilted her chin up to look at him. "And soon, you'll be coming too..."

He observed as her eyes deepened to a shadowy pine green; evidence that she was as equally aroused as he was.

She could almost feel his eyes searing her, the heat almost too much to bear. "Promise?" she asked flirtatiously.

With his fingertips still supporting her chin, he

gently brushed his mouth across the surface of her lips. "Uh-huh", he whispered against her mouth. "And I *always* keep my promises..."

Unable to ignore the pulsing need overwhelming her body, she rose onto her toes and took control of the kiss. Cupping his face, she assaulted his tongue with fierce desperation. She could feel her body losing control; sense the tension melting away. For the first time in her life, her mind and her body existed in perfect harmony.

And for the first time, she wasn't afraid of the repercussions.

Her aggressiveness threatened his sanity. He'd purposely held back, afraid if he moved too fast, came on too strong, he'd only push her away. He hadn't expected her to unleash such unbridled desire. Her hungry kiss communicated urgency; radiated an intense sensual energy.

Soft whimpers fled her mouth. Grant swallowed them, relishing the sound, savoring her lack of restraint. Her fingertips traveled down the distinct wall of his chest, further down the ripples of his six-pack abs, until she reached the fly of his navy cargo pants. She cupped and caressed his hard length, threatening to prematurely entice his release.

Gripping her wrists, he broke the kiss, resting his forehead against hers. "Slow down, baby. We've got all night."

Olivia shook her head. "I don't want to slow down. I need you; I don't want to wait anymore. *Please, Grant... please...*"

Picking her up, he tossed her onto the bed and before her body was able to bounce, he came down on top of her. Trailing kisses down her neck, he cupped one of her breasts, gently fondling her pink pebbled nipple with his thumb. And when his tongue mimicked what his thumb had just done, she arched her back, pressing her sensitive nipple deeper into his mouth.

Reaching down with his free hand, he gently glided his fingers against her slick, dewy center. "Is this for me, Livvy?" he asked, his voice rough and gritty as though he'd swallowed sandpaper. "Huh?—is this what I do to you?"

"Yes—*omigod!*" she gasped as he entered her body with one of his fingers.

Although her eyes were closed, she could feel him watching her, taking pleasure in her writhing body. *"Grant, please... I'm begging you!"*

His fingers never wavered. "Tell me what you want", he demanded softly.

"You—inside me—right now... *Please!*"

He planted his feet on the floor, removing his cargo pants and boxer briefs. He unrolled a condom over his throbbing length with lightening speed and then tugged her ankles, dragging her body to the edge of the bed. Standing above her, he wrapped her legs around his waist and braced his hands on either side of her head on the bed.

And then, he plunged into her...

His rigid girth filled her completely, her body stretching to accommodate the welcomed intrusion.

Hovering above her, his eyes raked across the surface of her feminine curves as their bodies collided. "God, Livvy, you're so beautiful."

He was close, his body dangling over the edge, and if his memory served him right, the sounds emanating from her indicated she was close, too.

Pleading whimpers.

Soft sensual moans.

Swift shallow breaths.

He'd never felt such a strong connection like this before. And that's when he realized—

—This wasn't just sex. He wasn't just filling a physiological need. For the first time in his life, he was making love...

With her eyes shut, her body was spiraling into a dark tunnel. The deeper she descended, the more pleasurable it became. She wanted the free fall to end, wanted the torturous exhilaration to stop, yet somehow the thought of ecstasy discontinuing left her panicked.

"Open your eyes. I want to see you", he breathlessly commanded.

Opening her eyes, she peered into his and at that moment, her body unleashed a shockwave of incandescent heat. Her body pulsed with powerful precision; every nerve-ending, every cell, from the top of her head to the tip of her pale pink pedicured toes.

Olivia called out his name and raked her nails over his back as her body released the tension. Her tight heat contracted around his rigid girth, gripping and releasing, causing his hard length to spasm. Staring into the eyes of the woman he loved, he emptied his essence, wishing the latex barrier no longer confined him.

Olivia rose onto her elbows and smiled, still panting from her climax. "Oh my gosh, Grant... Let's do that again..."

With their bodies finally sated, they invaded

the kitchen to satisfy their appetite. Olivia spooned vanilla frozen yogurt into two bowls and topped each with a handful of *Reese's Pieces* and a large puddle of chocolate syrup.

"Looks delicious", he said as he wrapped his strong arms around her from behind.

"Why, thank you! I guess I should confess: I have a weakness for this."

Grant nuzzled his face in the crook of her neck. "A weakness for my hands on you?" he asked as he spread gentle kisses across her skin.

Olivia smiled as she tilted her head, giving him better access. "That, too, but I was talkin' about the dessert."

"Oh—*that*..."

Turning to face him, she rose onto her toes and wrapped her arms around his neck. She playfully rubbed her nose against his several times before planting a quick kiss on his lips. "C'mon, we can eat in front of the TV."

Their bowls lay empty in front of them as they watched Jay Leno on *the Tonight Show*. Grant couldn't remember if he'd ever felt this happy, this content. Making love to Olivia was amorous, electrifying—*amazing*. But even more amazing was that she hadn't pushed him away.

Instead of retracting into herself like she had the first time they'd been intimate, she'd opened up. She'd trusted him enough to release her guard, exposing her vulnerable heart to him for the first time. He was honored at the gesture—her actions making him fall harder, deeper in love with her.

When the credits rolled, he knew it was time to leave her. He didn't want to—they'd reached a new milestone in their relationship—making substantial forward progress. He wanted so badly to believe the momentum would continue.

But what if it didn't? He didn't want to wake in the morning to find that the unguarded Livvy he left tonight was long gone.

"What are you thinkin' about?" she asked, interrupting his trance.

"What?—oh, nothing."

"It's definitely something", she said as she brushed her fingertips against his forehead. "You're makin' lines on your forehead—don't you know that causes premature wrinkles?"

Grant laughed in spite of himself. "Well, we wouldn't want that, now would we?"

Olivia pursed her lips together and stroked her chin as though she was deep in thought. "I don't know, Womack. Wrinkles on you would probably still be sexy."

"Is that right?"

"Yeah, I think so", she whispered before pressing her lips against his.

"Thank you for tonight", he confessed as he brushed a strand of hair away from her face. "It couldn't have been more perfect."

"I feel the same way", she uttered softly.

Standing up, he reached for his navy T-shirt and put it back on. After planting one last kiss on her voluptuous pink lips, he promised to call her the following morning, and then turned toward the door.

When she was finally alone, she released a gratifying sigh. Tonight had been perfect. In fact, she couldn't wait to close her eyes tonight and relive each tantalizing moment again in her dreams...

But first, she needed to start the dishwasher.

Reluctantly, she stood from the couch again and gathered the two bowls. She ambled toward the sink, rinsing them first before placing them in the dishwasher. She'd just started the cycle when she suddenly heard a knock at the door.

She smiled as she pivoted, her heart racing at the thought of Grant coming back to satisfy their desire again. "Forget something?" she shouted as she untwisted the lock.

But when she opened the front door, it wasn't Grant.

In front of her stood a tall, muscular man dressed in black, his face shielded by a dark ski mask...

CHAPTER 15

Olivia's gut twisted like a pretzel the moment she opened the door to find the masked arsonist standing before her. And then her adrenaline kicked-in. She shoved the door, but it was too late. The intruder had anticipated her move and had already placed his hands in front of him to catch it; then he lunged forward.

RUN!

If she could make it into the kitchen and grab her cell phone on the counter, she could exit through the French doors and lock herself in the darkroom...

Pivoting, she sprinted toward the bar. She made it halfway before the masked man grabbed a handful of her hair and yanked her back toward him.

"Where do you think you're going, Blondie?" He asked.

Olivia raised her arms, trying to disentangle his fingers from her hair as he hauled her to the living room like a cavewoman. She kicked her legs, attempting to get back on her feet, but he was pulling

her too quickly. A piercing scream fled her mouth—
but that only made him tug harder.

When he finally had her in the living room, he
launched her body forward. She gasped in agony as
her right side collided against the glass-top coffee
table, her body landing on a blanket of shattered
glass.

She tried to stand up—tried to get away. Once
she was on all fours, the mysterious man picked her
up as though she weighed nothing, and then tossed
her onto the red leather couch.

It was hard to breathe. Her ribs had struck the
table first, taking the brunt of the impact. She knew
they were most likely broken, but ironically she
didn't feel the pain—there was too much adrenaline
coursing through her veins. He came down on top of
her, straddling her abdomen to keep her from
running away.

I don't want to die—not like this!

She knew she had to fight back.

With her arms flailing about and her legs
kicking, she wriggled beneath him trying to set
herself free. But he was so much stronger than her.
By pure luck, her fist landed against his left temple.
The thick knit material of his ski mask cushioned
much of the blow, but she prayed it was enough to
make him realize she was not giving up.

"You fucking bitch!"

His hands clamped down on her wrists. He
raised her arms over her head, holding them in place
with a firm grip. And when he was able to pin her
flailing limbs with his vice-like grasp, he reared back
with his gloved, free hand and slapped her across the
face. The impact forced her head to the side, her

cheek on fire as though she'd been stung by a hundred bees.

"Now that I have your undivided attention, tell me where your camera is."

"Fuck you!" she yelled.

Olivia clenched her eyes shut as he reared his hand again. She expected him to slap her like he had moments earlier, but he didn't. Instead, his closed fist struck her mouth. Warm liquid exploded from her lips, the distinct metallic taste of blood on her tongue.

Arms pinned above her head, she opened her eyes to find he was inches away from her face.

"Maybe some other time", he whispered as his free hand copped a feel of one of her breasts.

Refusing to fall victim to the masked intruder any longer, she bucked and twisted her body, convulsing until she managed somehow to wriggle free. She rolled off the couch and then quickly planted her feet to run away.

This was harder than he'd thought it would be. She was tough. When he pushed, she pushed right back. No way was she going to give up, he acknowledged.

As soon as she'd made it to her feet, she'd lunged toward the kitchen. He couldn't let her get away.

He had to get his hands on that camera and any photos she may have already developed.

And he refused to leave without them.

He reached for the silver metal vase beside him on the end table and just like he'd done in high school as the quarterback of the football team, he launched the heavy vase toward the back of her fleeing head.

She could see her phone on the bar—just a few more strides and she could call for help.

WHACK.

Misery unlike anything she'd ever felt before radiated from the back of her head, her vision obscured by floating bright lights. Her legs collapsed beneath her as though she'd been tranquilized, her body landing just shy of the slate tile in the kitchen.

Touchdown...

Slowly he ambled toward her, the nasty gash on the crown of her head bleeding profusely, signifying the end to their struggle. He knelt down beside her and listened as she groaned in unyielding agony. It wasn't supposed to be like this. He didn't want to hurt her, but he needed to cover his tracks. Because if he didn't, it was only a matter of time before the police came knocking on his door, and even jail couldn't save him from the wrath his bookie would unleash.

He scanned the room and immediately noticed the camera on the opposite side of the bar near the range top. Standing, he stepped over her battered body and reached for it.

"I sure am sorry 'bout all this, Blondie", he said as he quickly cased the rest of the house for more incriminating pictures. *"Things would've turned out much better for you if you'd only cooperated."*

Satisfied that he'd collected what he came for, he knelt down beside her again, placing his lips inches away from her ear for emphasis. *"Why don't you make yourself useful: pose that pretty lil' ass in front of the camera instead of sneaking around, taking pictures of me. Stay out of my way or next time, things might not turn out so well for you..."*

Quietly, he stood up and walked to the front door, but before he turned the knob, he had one last bit of advice: *"Consider yourself warned."*

Olivia awoke on the floor. The moment she opened her eyes, raw, unbearable pain consumed her. She wasn't aware how long she'd been lying there, but she did know she needed to get help.

She attempted to get up, but her extremities felt like overcooked noodles. Although her vision was blurred, she scanned the room and suddenly remembered the horrific attack she'd endured. The living room looked as though a tornado had rushed past: broken glass littered the hardwood floor, books had fallen from the shelf adjacent to the TV. And she couldn't overlook the obvious: she was lying in a puddle of her own blood.

What if her attacker was still here? How on earth would she find the strength to fight back?

A wave of nausea came over her.

She was so tired. Weak.

Her body ached and her head threatened to explode. She dragged her body several feet through the agonizing pain.

Her eyelids were heavy.

Her body went limp.

And then, darkness...

Ty whistled as he shut the mailbox, flipping through the various pieces of junk mail while he strolled to the front door. Last night had been a good night at the station. He'd been able to sleep without interruption, the arsonist clearly taking a night off from his quest to torch the town, one random building at a time.

Reaching into his pocket, he grabbed his keys. Having lived here for the past eighteen years, he wasn't used to locking his front door. Butler Island was probably one of the safest places in America— nothing ever happened here. But with Olivia back in town, she'd insisted. She'd lived in New Orleans basically since she'd graduated college and although the famous city had an overall false reputation for high crime, it certainly wasn't a place one would forego precautionary measures.

Tucking the negligible mail under his arm, he fumbled with his keys until he came upon the correct one. Holding it between his thumb and first finger, he raised his hand to insert it into the lock, and then paused—

The door was cracked open several inches.

He had to admit the discovery was a bit odd; Olivia was adamant about locking the door— especially the nights she stayed here alone when he was on shift. But maybe she was finally beginning to realize how silly the whole thing was; breaking and entering was about as likely here as a white Christmas.

Ty nudged the door open, ready to give his baby sister a hard time about her blunder, when he stumbled into a home in complete disarray.

Books had fallen from the shelves, one of the table lamps had crashed to the ground, and a thick layer of glass scattered the floor around the coffee table.

"Olivia!" he shouted as he dropped the meaning-less mail from his arm. He came around the sofa, panic coursing through his veins as he acknowledged the struggle that'd taken place.

And that's when he saw it.

In two swift strides, Ty lunged toward the puddle of blood in front of the bar and followed the smeared trail further into the kitchen. Olivia's battered body lay motionless on the cold slate tile.

"Holy shit, Olivia!" he cried as he collapsed by her side.

Unaware of the extent of her injuries, he checked for a pulse...

She was alive!

"Olivia, can you hear me?" His training as a paramedic taught him not to move potential victims until their head and neck could be secured. She'd clearly suffered head trauma, the blood saturating her hair evidence of that.

He heard a raw groan escape her as she awoke. "Don't move, baby girl", he uttered as he reached into his pocket for his cell phone. After dialing 911, exchanging the necessary information on her condition, he covered the receiver with his free hand. Olivia was suddenly conscience and obviously disoriented as she attempted to raise her head.

"It's alright, baby girl, you're safe now."

"Ty?" she asked in a voice so weak, she wondered if she'd spoken aloud or merely imagined it.

"That's right, I'm here. You're gonna be alright. I just need you to be still for a few more minutes until we can secure your head and neck to the backboard."

"I'm hurtin', Ty."

"I know. Just a few more minutes and we'll have you lying in a comfortable bed with medication to take away the pain."

And then the search would begin for the sick bastard that did this to her. He just better hope the police found him before Ty did...

CHAPTER 16

Shifting his weight in the chair, Ty removed his wallet from his back pocket and laid it on the tray next to Olivia's hospital bed. He'd been listening while his little sister repeated the story of her brutal attack for the third time to the detective in the room, each time his gut twisted, his hands clenched, and his heart ached.

What kind of man attacked a helpless woman?

A monster.

A monster that sets fires and stops at nothing to silence potential witnesses to his crimes; a devilish beast that lacked compassion; a soulless coward terrified of punishment.

Ty forced himself to look at her. The blood that'd stained her blond hair was long gone, but the cuts and bruises on her face remained.

Battle wounds.

He knew the physical damage would heal with time—it was the emotional trauma that worried him most.

"Excuse me, detective", the doctor announced as he stood by the door. "Miss Everitt needs to rest. Can we continue this another time?"

The detective closed his notepad and stuck his pen back into his shirt pocket. "No problem; I think we have enough information for now." He stood and then handed Olivia his card. "Thank you for your time, Olivia. If you can think of anything else, I'd like for you to give me a call. And I mean anything—no matter how insignificant it may seem to you—it may help the case."

Olivia smiled and nodded. "Yes sir."

He turned to leave and then stopped at the door. "Oh, and by the way, you shouldn't be alone. This guy is ruthless and unpredictable. Let's not give him another opportunity to finish what he started..."

Once the detective was gone, Ty searched Olivia's battered face. "You okay?" he finally asked.

"I'm fine, Ty."

"Okay, well, I'm gonna step out for a minute and talk to the doctor. I'll be right back", he said as he rose from his chair. Pointing his finger at her, he stood over her. "Now, don't you go anywhere, you hear?" Olivia smiled. He knew she'd appreciate his humor. When she saluted him, he journeyed to the door and slipped out in time to catch up with her doctor.

"Excuse me, Dr. Conrad, do you have a minute?"

"Of course, Ty, what can I do for you?"

Ty scratched his head. "Well, I was hoping you could explain the extent of Olivia's injuries."

Dr. Conrad hugged the chart he held close to his body and rocked back on his heels. "She sustained a mild concussion from the blow to her head and a small laceration from the impact. We were able to close that up nicely with a few staples. X-rays indicated no fractures on the skull, however we did discover a lateral rib fracture. Unfortunately there isn't anything we can do for that. It'll take approximately six to eight weeks for it to heal and I'll prescribe pain medication to keep her comfortable. Aside from that, she has a lot of small cuts and bruises—with time they'll heal as well."

Ty wiped his hand down his face and then crossed his arms. "She wasn't, um... he didn't rape her, did he?" he finally asked.

"Well, I can't say for certain. It appears as though she did have intercourse, but nothing consistent with a violent rape."

"What do you mean?"

"Her attacker was obviously very rough with her. If he had raped her, it probably would've been rough, too... Professionally, I'd say it was *possible*; personally, I'd say the intercourse was most likely consensual."

Ty released a breath he hadn't been aware he was holding and nodded to their longtime family doctor. "Thanks, Doc, I really appreciate you taking the time to talk."

Dr. Conrad placed his hand on Ty's shoulder and gave it a squeeze. "My pleasure, although I would've much rather have seen the two of you under different circumstances."

Placing his hands in his pockets, he nodded. "Yeah, me too..."

* * * * *

"Can you tell me the room number for Olivia Everitt?" Grant asked the kind elderly woman sitting behind the hospital information desk. He waited as she cautiously pecked at the keyboard in front of her with her two index fingers, fighting the urge to leap over the counter and type the name himself.

"She's on the second floor in room"—putting on her eye glasses, she leaned forward—"room 224."

"Thanks", he said as he pivoted and rushed toward the elevator.

Luckily the elevator door was just opening as he approached. He waited for the passengers to exit before boarding and then impatiently pressed the button to transport him to the second floor several times before the door finally closed. His mind was racing. He didn't really know what to expect when he saw her. He only knew she probably looked a lot different from the woman he'd left last night.

The door slid open and immediately he saw Kendall, Chief Handler, and several guys from the fire department sitting in the waiting area. News like this certainly traveled fast, he thought.

Stepping off the elevator, he swallowed the mass of emotions threatening to expose him. Afraid if anyone looked too close, they'd realize he was a crazed maniac... *for Olivia.*

He was madly in love with her. He'd left her house just after midnight, endorphins flooding his body with a high so spellbinding—so heavenly—he'd questioned whether he'd actually died and went to heaven. But the euphoria had quickly dissipated when he'd received a frantic call from Ty this morning, stating that Olivia had been hurt—badly— and was admitted to Mainland Hospital.

He'd immediately rushed here, his mind accelerating faster than his speeding truck.

What'd happened? Would she be alright?

Kendall turned around as she heard the elevator open and observed Grant. He was consumed with panic, worry, and something else.

Love.

As if he'd realized how transparent he'd been, he suddenly suppressed it. "Grant", she called out as he stepped forward.

"How is she?" he asked.

Kendall met him halfway. "She's... she's okay."

"Where's Ty?"

"Over there", she said as she pointed down the hall, "talking to Dr. Conrad—"

The words had barely left her lips before he turned and rushed toward Ty. Dr. Conrad had already walked away, leaving his distraught best friend alone to reflect on the events that'd occurred.

"Ty, what the hell happened?" he asked frantically when he was finally within earshot.

"Some sick bastard broke into the house late last night and beat the shit out of my baby sister!" Moisture clouded Ty's eyes, the weight of the gruesome attack finally overwhelming his strong façade.

"Someone broke in?"

Ty ran his hand through his dark blond hair. "Well, actually, no. The son of a bitch knocked—and Liv didn't find it *odd* that somebody was knocking at the door at one o'clock in the morning—so she answered it. *He ambushed her at the door!*"

Grant closed his eyes. He tried to imagine how terrified she must've been, tried to comprehend how a man could lay his hand on a woman. When Grant opened his eyes, Ty's hands were cupped around his mouth, fighting to regain his composure.

"My lil' sister is tough, though. She fought with every ounce of strength she had—all one hundred twenty pounds of her! I... I found her this morning lying on the kitchen tile—she'd been there all night— too weak to move!"

"What did Dr. Conrad say? She gonna be alright?" *God, please let her be alright!*

Ty nodded. "Yeah, she's banged-up pretty bad, but it could've been a hell of a lot worse."

"What about the son of a bitch that did this to her—any idea what his motive was? Does he get-off on slapping women around or was he after something?"

Ty shook his head and shoved his hands in his pockets. "It was our boy."

"*Our boy?* What do you mean?"

"The arsonist."

"*What?* How can you be sure he's—*shit*—he knows about the pictures Olivia took, doesn't he?"

Ty nodded. "Yeah. After he knocked her unconscious, he stole her new camera. He even searched the house and took the pictures she'd printed of him. Told her to quit sneaking around—taking pictures of him—or else he'd be back."

Grant relaxed his clenched fists and took a deep breath. The phone call he'd received earlier from Ty had his panicked mind simulating all sorts of scenarios. But none of them were as horrific as reality...

"You look like shit, man", he said as he slapped Ty on the back. "Why don't you go to the cafeteria and get yourself a coffee and something to eat?"

Ty glanced over his shoulder at Olivia through the small window. "Can't. I don't want to leave her by herself."

"I'll sit with her. Go—she needs you to be strong for her."

With a heavy sigh, he managed a wry smile. "Thanks, bro. I'd really appreciate that."

Grant steeled himself with a deep breath before he quietly nudged the door open. Olivia was lying with her head turned toward the view from her second story window, so enthralled by the movement of the swaying palm trees, she hadn't noticed him. He took the opportunity to observe her for a moment, hoping to eliminate the look of shock from his face by the time she became aware of his presence.

"She's banged-up pretty bad, but it could've been a hell of a lot worse", Ty had said moments earlier. Looking at her bruised and battered body, he acknowledged if it *had* been much worse, she'd probably be dead...

She had Gauze wrapped around her head to hold the bandage on the crown of her head securely in place. A large bruise on her left cheek stained her flawless complexion and her kissable pouty lips were slightly swollen, her bottom lip blemished with a small gash.

Her attacker had clearly struck her with his fist, the realization caused Grant's fists to clench again. He wanted to kill the son of a bitch that did this to her with his bare hands; wanted to witness him gasping for his last breath.

His eyes continued their journey. He was unable to see underneath her gown, but he did notice that both her hands were wrapped in a light dressing. His heart convulsed with grief as rage like he'd never known before accumulated inside of him, threatening to explode every time he looked at her battered body. But now wasn't the time for that.

She was alive.

He swallowed the uproar internally consuming him and forced a smile. There'd be plenty of time to endure the internal fury engulfing him later.

"You need a new nickname", he said as he took a step toward her. Olivia turned her head to meet his gaze. "I think *Super Woman* suits you much better."

She smiled as much as her swollen lips would allow. "You know me: I'm just an adrenaline junkie lookin' for my next high! After that Ferris wheel ride, I needed another rush. Guess I need to watch what I wish for, huh?"

Reaching for the extra chair wedged in the corner, he hauled it close to her bedside and then took a seat. After loosely intertwining her bandaged hand in his, he raised them to his lips and kissed the back of it. "You look beautiful", he began.

Olivia released a gut-busting laugh and then winced as she clutched her broken rib with her freehand. "Don't make me laugh—it hurts", she demanded, grinning. She examined his face as he furrowed his brow.

"He didn't, um", Grant swallowed, "you weren't—"

"Raped?" she asked. "No", she uttered as she shook her head, "he was far too busy slappin' me around."

Grant released a breath he hadn't been aware he was holding as relief washed over him. At least she'd been spared that. Running his fingers through his hair, he slid to the edge of his seat.

He was struggling for control; she could see it in his body language, in his eyes. Uncomfortable with anyone making a fuss over her, she did what she'd always done: depict the carefree attitude she'd perfected years ago. "I'm okay, Grant, really. Everything is gonna be fine."

Grant met her gaze. "Don't do that, baby", he uttered softly.

"Don't do what?"

"Try to comfort me—that's what I'm supposed to be doing for you..."

Ty made it halfway to the cafeteria before he realized he'd left his wallet behind in Olivia's room. Pivoting, he boarded the elevator again, too exhausted to take the stairs. He pinched the bridge of his nose and clenched his eyes shut during the brief ascent.

He still expected to wake any moment and discover that the nightmare he'd endured since stumbling upon his battered little sister this morning was just that: a nightmare.

He knew better.

How many times had he pinched himself this morning in an attempt to waken?

Too many.

In fact, if he didn't stop, he'd end up with bruises all over his body, too!

The bell from the elevator quickly brought him back to reality and when the door slid open, he drifted toward room 224. Quietly he opened the door, unsure if she'd finally succumbed to exhaustion. He didn't want to wake her—she needed her rest. Voices indicated otherwise and that's when he overheard...

"I can't help but feel responsible for all this", Grant said as he waved his free hand over her body.

"Grant, this isn't your fault—"

"I should've stayed with you longer. If I wouldn't have left when I did, this probably wouldn't have happened."

"The detective believes the man that did this was most likely watchin' the house, waitin' for the perfect opportunity for me to be alone. It wouldn't have mattered when you left—he still would've been there waitin'..."

"When did this happen?—how long after I left?" he inquired.

Olivia shrugged her sore shoulders. "I don't know—five—ten minutes?"

Closing his eyes, he sighed. "Damn it, Livvy, when I got the call that you'd been hurt, I—"

"Look at me", she demanded as she gently squeezed his hand. "I'm only gonna say this one more time, okay? It. Wasn't. Your. Fault. I'm gonna be just fine. I may look like a complete mess right now, but with a little make-up and a cute outfit, nobody will ever suspect I suffered any injuries!"

And let's not forget a little humor, she thought. That had been her longtime secret weapon against emotional trauma from her past.

When you don't have the strength within you— fake it. Because if she couldn't overcome her personal struggles, she could at least gain satisfaction from comforting those that surrounded her.

"You're amazing, you know that?" he said smiling.

"Why, yes, I do—I've been told that a time or two", she explained as she gave him a playful wink.

Amazing didn't even begin to describe how he felt about her, he acknowledged. Her strength was contagious; he wanted to be strong—for her. He couldn't think of another person who could lie there and make light of their circumstances. Her attacker may have inflicted physical damage to her beautiful body, but at least he hadn't broken her spirit.

Ty quietly closed the door.

"I'd say the intercourse was most likely consensual", Dr. Conrad had said earlier. He'd been so relieved to hear she hadn't been raped, he'd over-looked the obvious: she'd had sex before her attack. Before her attack she'd been with Grant—*his best friend fucked his lil' sister!*

No—no that couldn't be, could it?

No—it *had* to be someone else. Grant and Olivia were *friends*—that's all.

But sometimes the way Grant looked at her, Ty wondered if maybe they *were* more than friends...

Inhaling a deep cleansing breath, he raised his hand to the door, knocked twice, and then opened it. Startled, Grant removed his hand from Olivia's and then leaned back in his chair.

"Back so soon?" Grant asked.

Ty stepped into the room and walked toward the tray on the other side of Olivia's bed. "Got halfway there and then realized I forgot my wallet."

Once he had it in his grasp, he eyed Grant suspiciously for a several seconds and then asked, "Can I get anyone anything?"

When both Grant and Olivia shook their heads, he started for the door. "I'll be back in a few minutes—sorry to interrupt."

Grant watched as Ty closed the door behind him. There was no mistake about it: he knew about his relationship with Olivia. The bold stare and the "sorry to interrupt" comment were evidence of that.

He glanced at Olivia; she appeared as though she was too exhausted to have noticed and mentioning it to her now would only upset her. Things were about to get real interesting on Butler Island.

A very dangerous man was on the loose and once he was caught, Grant was pretty sure that Ty would be coming after him next...

CHAPTER 17

It's show time, Olivia thought as she sat in the living room, surrounded by loved ones. She'd been home from the hospital for three days and was already uncomfortable with the attention she'd received from the worried residents of Butler Island.

Her childhood home had become a revolving door: neighbors, friends, as well as members of her extended family at the fire department, had all made an effort to visit. In fact, she'd barely had a moment of privacy since Ty had discovered her almost a week ago, lying in a pool of her own blood on the cold slate tile.

Today's performance was of utmost importance: Kendall and Grant—the two people who knew her best aside from Ty—were flanked on either side of her, staring at her as though she were a house of cards on the verge of collapse. Their careful scrutiny was cumbersome, uncomfortable. Exuding strength and confidence would hopefully put everyone's mind at ease—*including her own.*

She hadn't seen Grant in three days, his absence further signifying just how important he had become in her life. They'd spoken every day, but she'd missed his smile, his warmth, his touch. With Ty observing every breath she took, every move she made, they'd decided that distance would prevent speculation about their relationship.

Sensing her need to be alone with him, Kendall spoke up. "Ty, do you think you can show me what your daily routine is in regards to caring for your pool?" she asked as she twirled a silky strand of black hair around her manicured fingers. "I've been thinking about getting an above ground pool for my backyard this spring."

"Now?" he asked incredulously.

"Uh-huh—I mean, if it's not too much trouble..."

Ty was in awe of the beauty before him. Her ink-black hair settled around her shoulders, glistening under the lamp's intimate glow. Two large amber eyes nearly pinned him with their intense gaze, and plump rose lips turned upward in a radiant smile, caressing the depths of his broken soul; mending him from the inside out. Clearing his throat, he offered his hand. "No trouble at all."

Grant eyed them as they advanced toward the French doors. The look of admiration didn't escape him: Ty was clearly attracted to Kendall. But it seemed to be more than that.

He'd stood by as his best friend mourned the end of his marriage. There was no doubt that Cameron's sudden departure created an unimaginable void in Ty's life. He'd loved that woman more than she'd deserved and when she left, she'd taken his soul with her.

For the first time in recent memory, he recognized life behind Ty's green eyes...

And lust. Maybe there was hope for him after all.

Grant waited until they were out of sight before turning toward the beauty beside him. "How're you doing, *really?*"

Sighing, she answered, "I'm okay. Having a little trouble sleeping, but other than that..."

Reaching for her hand, he ran his thumb against her palm as if trying to read her. "The cuts are healing nicely."

"Apparently, *Super Woman* has super healin' powers."

Chuckling softly, he tucked her hair behind her ear. "I've missed you like crazy the last few days."

Olivia tore her eyes away from their joined hands and peered into his ice-blue gaze. His admission floored her. It wasn't necessarily the words that'd shocked her; she knew he'd missed her. It was the way he'd said them—like he would've died if he'd had to wait a minute longer to see her, like he'd wither away if not for the warmth of her body next to his. And if that weren't shocking enough, she realized that his absence had created a longing unlike anything she'd ever experienced before, too.

"Ditto", she replied, unable to articulate the mounting emotions threatening to fracture her guarded heart.

"So with Ty going back to work tomorrow, what are you gonna do?"

"Well, if it were up to me I'd stay here, but my overprotective big brother refuses to compromise on that."

"And I agree with him on that—you shouldn't be alone."

"Looks like I'll be seeing you at the fire station tomorrow, and as for tomorrow night... He's planning on having Lieutenant Hudson cover his overnight shift."

"Seems like he's got it all figured out then."

"Honestly", she began, "I think everyone is overreactin'. I'm a big girl—I can take care of myself."

"Honey, nobody's questioning your capabil-ities—*or your courage*—for that matter. It's your safety that concerns us."

"I understand that, but... the man that did this... well, surely he wouldn't be stupid enough to come back...?"

Cupping the back of her neck, he ran his callused thumb along her cheek. "The arsonist is obviously afraid of being caught and with your pictures exposing him in the act, he most likely felt you were a threat. Trying to probe the mind of a maniac and rationalize his choices and decisions isn't my expertise. But I can guarantee one thing: any man that hits a woman is a coward. He waited until you were alone and defenseless—that won't happen again. We're not gonna give him the opportunity to hurt you a second time."

Olivia ran her fingers through her hair and released a heavy sigh. "Why does this kind of stuff always happen to me? *Damn it!* I feel like my entire life I've been trying to outrun an endless black cloud—one tragedy after the next—"

Before he could question the meaning behind her statement, Ty and Kendall emerged from the patio, their laughter and flirtatious interplay an indication that they'd most likely strayed from "Pool Upkeep 101."

"You know what?" Olivia announced as she rose from the couch. "I think I'm gonna take a nice, hot shower…"

Grant eyed Olivia as she walked away. There was something different about her demeanor. She'd been seconds away from revealing the pain from her past, and her sudden urge to take a hot shower was merely a cover.

Olivia paused just before reaching the hall, looking over her shoulder. "Thank you both for stoppin' by", she said as she pasted her *"everything-is-fine smile."*

Who did she think she was fooling? He wondered. It'd been just over two months since he'd stumbled upon her at the beach and in that time, he'd been given the opportunity to get to know her well. *He knew her*, knew that the smile she unveiled moments before disappearing down the hall wasn't genuine—it was forced. It lacked the radiance he was use to, exposing the bone-deep agony she kept hidden so eloquently.

He prayed that the brilliance would return to her emerald eyes, prayed that her contagious spirit would prevail. He couldn't take away her pain, but he could love her. And that's exactly what he planned on doing.

Following the orders of her overprotective sibling, Olivia arrived at the fire station the following morning with a carefree smile adorned to her nearly healed face and an old outdated 35mm camera in tow. She'd spent the better part of the day observing the everyday happenings at the fire station: washing the fire engine, performing various training exercises, preparing lunch. She'd captured the "brotherhood" behind the scenes; the moments that the general public weren't at privy to see.

The fire station had always felt like home. She'd always felt a part of this family—an extended member. But today... today she was a part of the "brotherhood", too.

The realization hit her like a ton of bricks.

This was her family.

Olivia thought back to the theater fire. She had been seconds away from witnessing a living nightmare: a roof collapse with four men she cared about still inside. Thankfully they'd escaped unharmed. But what about the next time?

Closing her eyes, she tried to push the thoughts from her head. The arsonist had to be caught—soon. Because although she was a master at exuding courage and strength, she knew she lacked the fortitude to mourn another loss.

Grunting, Grant pushed the heavy weighted barbell away from his broad chest and secured it in place. Lifting weights had always served two particular purposes: it kept his body in shape and kept his mind clear. Today he was lifting for the latter.

Having Olivia here at the fire station was bittersweet. He was partially at ease with the knowledge that she was safe, but as always was the case with Olivia, the constant need to touch her consumed him.

How many times had he lost his focus in a vivid reverie?

Too many.

How often had he clenched his fists to keep himself from reaching for her when she strolled by?

Too often.

How frequently had he bit his tongue to prevent himself from telling her exactly how he felt about her?

Too frequently.

Before he could further psychoanalyze his mind, Ty waltzed into the small weight room. Without uttering a word, he stepped onto the treadmill wedged in the corner and began a slow jog. Rising from the bench, Grant reached for his towel and wiped the moisture from his face and neck, Ty's steady glare boring holes into him.

"Everything alright?" Grant finally asked.

"It's nothing."

"Bullshit—what's up?"

Ty hesitated for a few long beats. "Just got into it with Liv."

Grant sat back down on the edge of the bench and leaned his forearms on his knees. "About...?"

"Larry was supposed to cover my shift tonight, but his wife got called in at the hospital. Apparently there's a shortage of nurses", he explained wryly. "I cleared it with Chief Handler and then told Liv she'd have to bunk here tonight... Let's just say she didn't take the news very well."

"Well, in her defense, she's a grown woman— capable of making her own decisions."

Ty slammed his hand on the stop button, abruptly ending his leisurely run, and then leapt off the treadmill. "Yeah, speaking of *'decisions'*, whose idea was it to sneak behind my back a begin dating my sister?

Grant stood from the bench and watched as Ty advanced toward him. "It wasn't like that—"

"Really?" he questioned as he invaded Grant's personal space. "You don't have the best reputation with women, bro." To give his next point emphasis, he pointed his index finger and jabbed it into Grant's sternum. "You're *exactly* the kind of guy she doesn't need in her life!"

Suppressing the urge to ram his fist down Ty's throat, he inhaled a deep cleansing breath. "Again, it wasn't like that. We—"

"So you're gonna stand here and deny that you fucked my little sister...?" Ty watched as Grant looked away. Of course he wasn't going to deny it—he was a lot of things, but he wasn't a liar. "Yeah... that's what I figured..." Ty took a step back and then turned to walk away.

"She's not just another girl, Ty... She's *different.*"

With his back still turned, Ty shoved his hands in his pockets. "Yeah, I know. She's had one hell of a life—endured more tragedy in twenty-seven years than most folks experience in a lifetime. She's *very different...*"

"So, what about tonight?" Grant asked curiously.

Finally turning around to face him, he answered, "What about it?"

Grant wrapped the hand towel around his neck and tugged on the ends. "Well, she doesn't want to sleep here at the station and we both agree she shouldn't be alone... She can stay with me tonight—"

"Like hell she will!"

"Look, I know you're upset with me right now, but—"

"Upset? No, I'm not upset—*I'm fucking pissed!*"

Grant threw his hands up in surrender. "Fine—you're *'fucking pissed'* at me. But this isn't about you or me... It's about Olivia and keeping her safe." He observed his best friend: his clenched jaw and intense glare reflected anger, betrayal, contempt.

Ty ran his hand through his hair and replied through clenched teeth. "Fine. But do me a favor: keep your dick in your pants..."

CHAPTER 18

"You can put your bag in the last bedroom on the left", Grant said as he pointed down the hall. He'd made a brief pit stop at Olivia's after leaving the fire station to allow her the opportunity to pack an overnight bag. And then had set his sights on spending the evening alone with the woman he loved.

Olivia trekked down the hall and entered the last bedroom on the left...

Grant's room.

The hardwood floor creaked beneath her feet as she drifted toward the night stand. Setting her bag on the floor, her eyes skimmed the room. The walls were painted a deep blue-gray: the color of the sky just before a storm. The bed was covered in a crisp white comforter and on the opposite wall, a sliding glass door opened to the expansive deck.

It looked like a nautical paradise... Clean lines. No clutter—just the essentials. Her lips tilted in a smile. Waking up to this view would be conducive to her recovery—she just prayed that when

her head finally reached the pillow, the serene
environment would protect her from her hellish
nightmares...

Grant stood in the kitchen chopping vegetables
to toss into the stir fry he'd quickly thrown together,
his mind steadily focused on the woman he'd sent to
his bedroom. It felt good to have her here—like her
presence filled the emptiness in his house.

In his life.

Before he could delve into the seriousness of
his feelings, the beautiful "missing link" emerged
from the hall and joined him in the kitchen.

"Whatcha makin'?"

"Chicken stir fry. Hope you're hungry."

"Starving."

Grant spooned rice into two bowls and topped
it with the spicy chicken and vegetable mixture and
then motioned for her to step onto the deck. He followed behind, Dexter mirroring his movement, ready
to catch a bite with his salivating mouth in the event
that a piece of chicken spilled over the edges.

"Wow, this looks delicious!" She stated. "My
compliments to the chef!"

"Thanks."

"So, I'm curious. How *did* you manage to convince Ty that staying here was a good arrangement?"

Grant shrugged his shoulders, hoping he
appeared composed; his confrontation with Ty had
been anything but calm. "It wasn't that difficult,
really. He couldn't leave the fire station tonight; you
refused to stay there; I offered a solution."

"Yes, but—"

"We both have one common goal: your safety", he said directly. She winced at his surly tone and he immediately felt like an ass. "I'm sorry. I didn't mean for that to sound so—"

"Harsh?"

"Yeah, and rude..."

There was an awkward moment of silence between them before she finally spoke again. "So I'm here because you feel guilty about what happened to me?—is that it?"

Grant dropped his fork in his bowl and intertwined their fingers. How did he reassure the woman he'd fallen for how much he cared without mentioning the three words on the tip of his tongue? "You're here because I *want* you to be... Please tell me you believe that."

"I do now", she whispered.

The remainder of dinner felt more comfortable, their conversation casual and lighthearted compared to their earlier discussion. He'd even managed to make her laugh a bit, the sound reverberating through him like an elaborate symphony.

After their bowls were emptied they retreated back to the kitchen. Olivia placed her dish in the sink and then began gathering the wok and cutting board he'd used to prepare their meal.

"What do you think you're doing?"

"Cleanin' the kitchen."

"The hell you are!" he said as he retrieved the wok from her grasp.

"C'mon, Grant, I'm not helpless!" She explained.

"I never said you were."

Olivia crossed her arms and tilted her chin up to look at him. "Not directly, but that's what you're implying... C'mon, it's the least I can do for all you've done for me already."

Grant placed the wok in the sink and then reached for her. Giving in to his embrace, Olivia nestled against him, resting her forehead against his solid chest.

After placing a kiss on the top of her head, he tilted her chin with his fingertips. "I've got this. Why don't you take a shower, slip into something a little more comfortable and then meet me on the couch. I'll open a bottle of wine and we can watch a movie."

"Okay", she managed, just above a whisper.

Drifting down the hall, Olivia entered the bedroom and rummaged through her bag for her toiletries. Clutching the various bottles against her body, she toddled toward the bathroom and slowly removed her clothes.

Since her attack, she'd purposely refrained from looking at herself, her blemished skin a painful reminder of that horrific night. But standing in front of the full-length mirror attached to the back of the bathroom door, she allowed herself a peek. The bruises on her face, wrists, and torso had faded into a subtle shade of yellow-green and the cuts she'd sustained on her hands and knees were on the mend.

She barely recognized the woman staring back at her. She was alone—she didn't have to pretend. The expression on her face and the insecure gleam in her eyes frightened her.

Unable to view the spiritless form before her any longer, she stepped into the shower and drew the curtain. She stood underneath the blazing liquid, washing her hair and then her body. She scoured her skin until her flesh appeared pink, felt raw. But no matter how diligently she scrubbed, she couldn't cleanse her mind.

The masked ravager lurked in every dark corner of her conscious: stealing her soul, looting her liveliness, raiding her resolve. How had she managed to end up here again? How could she have allowed vulnerability to invade her being?

She barely felt the sting of scorching water streaming down her tender flesh as she rinsed the suds from her body, barely recalled the moment scalding moisture mingled with her tears. Overwhelmed with fear and despair, she leaned her back against the wall and slowly slid down until she sat on the floor of the tub, knees to her chest. Hugging her legs, she held on as the dam of emotions burst inside her. Sealed in a sauna, sheltered from prying eyes, she surrendered.

Finally finished in the kitchen, he opened a bottle of merlot and filled two glasses before replacing the cork. He probably should've told Olivia the truth: Ty knew about their relationship and needless to say, he wasn't thrilled. But Grant didn't want to upset her. She had enough worries, the last thing she'd needed was another burden to shoulder.

He wanted to protect her—not just from the maniac that'd attacked her—but from every source of anguish threatening her peace of mind. He'd gladly endure the physical and emotional pain she'd suffered if—

—Grant looked at his watch. It'd been thirty minutes since she'd disappeared from the kitchen to take a shower. Marching down the hall, he entered his bedroom and heard the water still running in the bathroom. As he journeyed further into his room, he heard something else, too: *the unmistakable sound of a grief-stricken woman, sobbing.*

"Olivia...? Everything alright...?" he called out. When there was no response, he turned the knob and gently nudged the door open. The sound of her sobs echoed against the walls of the small room, piercing his heart, infuriating his mind.

Through the transparent vinyl shower curtain, he saw her. "Livvy, baby", he uttered as he rushed toward the silhouette huddled on the floor of the bathtub. In one smooth motion, he quickly shoved the curtain out of his way and turned off the water.

The image of this beautiful woman huddled into a ball, arms wrapped around her legs, head resting on her knees, shoulders heaving as she released her tears, would forever be etched in his memory.

Despair had ravaged her so completely, she hadn't realized he was hovering above her until she felt his warm hands under her arms, lifting her to her feet.

"Damn it, Livvy!—you feel like an ice cube!" He realized that she'd been so blindsided by her emotions that she'd collapsed onto the floor of the tub and wept until the searing water had turned frigid, her mind in such turmoil, she hadn't noticed.

Reaching for a towel, he swaddled her in it and then swept her shivering body into his arms. Placing her on the edge of his bed, he knelt in front of her.

She was breaking his heart.

Grant peered into her red swollen eyes and gently brushed his knuckles against her bruised cheek. "Livvy, baby, talk to me..."

"I'm so sorry", she finally whispered.

"Baby, you have nothing to be sorry about... It's okay to cry."

Olivia shook her head in disagreement. *She didn't cry*—at least not in front of anyone. Tears were meant to be shed in private. "No, it's not—it's weak."

"Is that what you think?" he asked in disbelief. "Livvy, you're the strongest woman I've ever met. You've been through hell the last ten days. Crying *isn't* a sign of weakness—hell, I'd be worried if you didn't! Don't shut me out. *Talk to me...*"

Olivia hesitated at first; she wasn't accustomed to sharing her feelings—her fears. But somehow at that moment, *she felt safe.* "I can't get the image of him out of my head: the weight of him sittin' on me, his grasp around my wrists, the smell of whiskey on his breath..." Olivia closed her eyes as a single tear descended down her bruised cheek.

"Make me forget, Grant", she uttered softly.

Releasing the towel, it settled into a puddle around her waist and with both hands suddenly free, she cupped his face. She inched forward until she felt the warmth of his mouth against her icy lips.

Her lips were so cold. He told himself that the kiss was merely a way to increase her body temperature—nothing more. But as soon as her tongue collided against his, it was *his* temperature that rose—as well as other parts of his anatomy. He could almost taste her fear, her anguish and with every soft sweep of his tongue, the potency dissipated.

As much as he wanted her, as much as he wanted to steer her mind away from the monstrous memories that haunted her—he couldn't—not like this. He couldn't ignore his conscience. He repeatedly heard Ty's voice in his head, warning him to "keep his dick in his pants."

With every ounce of willpower he had, he covered her hands with his, peeling them away from his face, disconnecting their mating mouths.

"What's wrong?" she asked breathlessly. "Don't you want me?"

Grant eyed the angelic figure before him. Was she serious? Did she not see the hard bulge pressing against the fly of his navy cargos? "God, yes—"

"Then what's the problem?"

"I don't want to hurt you and this"—he said as he gestured to her naked body— "is not why I wanted you to stay with me tonight."

"So why *did* you want me to stay?"

"I needed to know you were safe. I couldn't live with myself if something happened to you again and... *I really missed you...*"

Olivia pinned him with her emerald gaze. Yes, it made her feel vulnerable, but she refused to dwell on it. Swallowing hard, she spoke the words envisioned in her mind. "I want to feel you, Grant—*I need to feel you.*"

Reaching for his hand, she placed it on her breast and sighed as his thumb caressed her pebbled nipple. "Save me", she uttered, just above a whisper. "Make me forget everything except how good you make me feel... *Please...*"

She was literally begging him to touch her. He'd tried to do the noble thing by ending their kiss—

But she was begging him...

His determination fractured; he gave in.

His lips skimmed the delicate skin on her neck

while his hands fondled her round breasts. She arched her back as he trailed kisses along her throat, down her chest. Her silk-like skin was perfumed with vanilla from her recent shower and like eating an ice cream cone, he licked the curve of her breast, savoring the flavor of her sweet damp skin on his tongue.

Continuing down her lovely figure, he came upon her broken rib. It was still bruised from her attack, her skin stained with a terrifying memory. Gently, he brushed his fingertips over the discoloration and then pressed a soft kiss against her battle wound; wishing his touch could mend her broken body and the emotional scars that would linger long after she healed.

His tenderness caused goosebumps to spread across her skin.

"You cold?" he uttered against her belly.

"No. Not anymore..." Her frozen body began to thaw the moment he'd put his mouth on her skin, melting her worries, her pain, and her fears like an ice sculpture in the sweltering dessert sun.

God, how he wanted to fill her with ecstasy; wanted to feel her moist heat clamp down on him. But he'd not only promised Ty he'd be on his best behavior, he'd also vowed to himself. He'd broken that pledge the moment he'd tasted her fragrant skin. He wanted to feast on her—pleasure her in the most intimate way—and he convinced himself once she'd experienced it, he'd stop.

"Lie back", he demanded in a soft, gravelly tone. Once she'd complied, he tugged on the back of her legs until her firm bottom teetered on the edge of the bed. Still kneeling in front of her, his shoulders pressed her knees apart, giving him a heavenly view. "God, look at you", he croaked.

He trailed kisses down the inside of her thigh, slowly inching toward her divine center. "I've wanted to do this since that first day on the beach", he mumbled against her leg. Unable to resist any longer, he put his mouth on her, savoring her sweet essence.

Her hips bucked the moment his mouth came down on her and in an effort to keep her still, he braced his forearm against them to keep her in place. "Mmmm...You taste so good, Livvy."

She'd never felt anything so erotic, so momentous. *So. Damn. Good.*

Her body was ablaze, heat accelerating over her—through her—like a fire storm. He devoured her until rationale was gone. Her body was possessed by a hidden sensual being, a distant part of herself that'd been buried deep within her. This man uncovered the hidden treasure... *Grant.*

"Grant!" She cried.

He couldn't get enough of her—never wanted to stop. He wanted more—needed more! Removing his arm from her hips, he slid his fingers underneath her firm bottom and lifted her closer.

She was panting his name, writhing in mindless pleasure, desperately balancing on the edge of climax.

"Come for me", he commanded hoarsely. Suddenly, he felt her fingers grip his hair; watched as her body twisted. He heard the sexiest carnal cry escape her and feasted on her pleasure as though it was his last meal.

Gently placing her bottom back onto the bed, he stood, bracing his hands on either side of her. He hovered for close to minute, simply watching—relishing.

When her breathing began to return to normal, she opened her eyes, allowing him a glimpse into her fragile soul. She wanted him—all of him—everything he was willing to give. And tonight—for one night—she would give him everything she had in return.

Her eyes never swaying from his gaze, she reached down and caressed him. The barrier of his cargo's hindering her effort, she dislodged the button and lowered the zipper.

"What're you doing?" he asked hoarsely.

Olivia tore one of her hands away and brought her finger to her lips. "Shhh." She returned her attention back to freeing his bulging length from confinement.

"This is probably not a good idea", he said as he braced himself above her.

"Why, Grant?" she whispered.

It was so hard to talk with her hands on him, so hard to think. "Because I— *God, Livvy",* he groaned as she gripped him, stroking him slowly, firmly.

"Please, Grant—I need this, too."

"I don't want to hurt you."

Staring into his blue bedroom eyes, she raked her teeth against her bottom lip. He loved it when she did that. She knew she wasn't playing fair. He was worried about her injuries; she needed to convince him otherwise. "The only way you're gonna hurt me is if you say no."

Every ounce of will he'd had left had been shattered. Who was he fooling? He couldn't resist this woman—not when she was completely naked beneath him—not when she gnawed on her bottom lip and looked at him with those angelic green eyes—and certainly not when she was begging for him to fill her with his love.

"Scoot back toward the headboard", he ordered softly before he had second thoughts.

Olivia followed his directions, resting her head on one of his feathery pillows. She observed as he stripped his clothing, his sinewy body causing her pulse to flutter. He ambled toward the nightstand, reaching for protection. And when his rigid sex was sheathed, he climbed into bed next to her.

"How should we do this?" she asked curiously.

"Turn away from me, on your side."

Olivia rolled onto her uninjured side and shivered when his sex pressed against her bottom.

"Are you sure you want to do this?" he asked as he spread soft kisses along the back of her shoulder.

"Yes, please."

Grant lifted her top leg and then slowly plunged into her slick tight heat.

"God, Livvy, I... I—"

I love you. More than anything, he wanted to confess. Wanted her to know how amazing she made him feel; wanted to hear her say those three words back. But that would probably be the dumbest move he'd ever make. He couldn't just blurt it out—that would have her retreating quicker than a striking viper snake.

Biting his lip, he relished her warm flesh; savored her sensual sounds. Thrusting into her body was like coming home.

And there was no place like it...

* * * * *

He stood on the deck, peeking around the edge of the sliding glass door. He ought to be out somewhere, scoping out his next target, but he couldn't peel his eyes away. Olivia fascinated him—always had.

She had more courage, more strength in her dainty lil' pinky finger than most guys did at the department. He really admired that about her.

Before the attack, he thought she was beautiful.

After the attack...?

Well, let's just say his fascination grew.

Silently, he cursed himself. He couldn't forget that she was a potential threat to his "part-time gig." After he'd left her house that night, he'd ransacked the place looking for equipment, pictures, film; anything that she'd need to begin photographing again.

He'd found an expensive camera, two lenses, and several pictures she'd printed of him in the act. Worried that Womack would return, he'd rushed out of there quickly.

Everything had been great—until she arrived this morning at the fire station with a small, ancient looking 35mm camera! He'd tried to warn her: told her she needed to pose instead of photographing. Apparently she'd disregarded his warning.

He needed to keep his eye on her; ensure she didn't regain the courage to come looking for him again. That should be easy; eyeing her was certainly no hardship.

But this time, he needed a new approach. He didn't *want* to hurt her again. Sitting at the hospital after her attack, he was disgusted with himself. He'd never hit a woman before; that was pretty low—even for him! He'd only meant to scare her; had hoped that his presence would've petrified her with fear.

Fear can cause a person to do unimaginable things—he of all people should know. He still owed his bookie two grand. How he'd managed to dig himself into a hole this deep, he'd never know. But he was damn well going to dig himself out of it. Three— maybe a half dozen more fires—was all he'd need in order to pay off his debt.

And then he'd be free.

But in the mean time, he'd continue looking over his shoulder; continue setting fires.

Continue his fascination with Olivia Everitt...

CHAPTER 19

She was running, desperately trying to escape. But he was too quick.

"Where do you think you're going, Blondie?" He asked.

He was dragging her by her hair; tears leaked from her eyes. Every time she screamed, he only tugged harder.

He shoved her.

A crushing pain blasted her side and sucked the air from her lungs like a vacuum.

Glass was everywhere. Shattered fragments pressed into her knees and the palms of her hands, slicing into her.

Blood. Pain.

Suddenly she was lying on the couch. He was sitting on her stomach, his weight holding her down. She had to fight back. She was so terrified—but she had to fight back! She kicked her legs; flailed her arms.

Victory! Her fist collided against his temple.

Oh no! He's angry!

He pinned her arms above her head. An elec-
trifying sting erupted against her cheek. Tears fled
her eyes again.

"Now that I have your undivided attention, tell
me where your camera is."

"Fuck you!" she yelled.

Another blow. Warm liquid exploded from her
mouth. She tasted blood on her tongue.

"Maybe some other time", he whispered.

His free hand copped a feel of one of her
breasts. She squirmed. Convulsed.

She had to get away from this monster!

Grant awoke to the sound of Olivia screaming.
She was having a nightmare.

Her arms were flailing and her body was
writhing as though she were in pain. The terror on
her face pulverized his heart. He gently pressed on
her shoulders, trying to calm her. "Livvy, it's okay.
It's just me... Grant."

He wanted to comfort her, assure her that she
was safe. But she was fighting him. One of her
flailing arms connected with his chin.

Olivia opened her eyes. It took her a few
moments before she realized what'd happened. The
room was dark, but a dim beam of moonlight that'd
filtered through the sliding glass door illuminated his
face enough for her to see.

Grant.

"I'm so sorry! I didn't mean to—"

"It's okay, baby. You're safe. It was just a bad
dream..."

Olivia reached up and ran her fingertips over

the course stubble along his chin. "I hurt you", she uttered softly.

"I'm fine—it's you I'm worried about... Do you wanna talk about it?" Olivia shook her head. Cupping her face, he whispered, "What can I do?"

"Just hold me..." Turning away from him, she nestled her back against the solid wall of his chest.

His heart ached for her. What he wouldn't give to erase the horrid memories of that night. What he wouldn't give to slay the demons that haunted her dreams. Olivia was selfless, compassionate, and courageous.

A fighter.

She would get past this with time; he truly believed that. But that didn't make witnessing her nightmares any easier. She didn't deserve this—no woman did—and he wished like hell he had the words to sooth her weary mind; the power to erase the horrid memories from that night.

Running his fingers through her hair, he glanced at his alarm clock: half past three. Her breathing had slowed, regaining a steady rhythm. He continued petting her, coaxing her into a deep, peaceful sleep. The love he felt for the woman in his arms threatening to burst.

"You still awake?" he whispered softly. He waited a few moments and when she didn't answer, the three words he'd never spoken to anyone before rolled off his tongue like an endearing caress. *"I love you..."*

She'd been lying in his arms, his magical hands caressing her hair, blanketing her body in safety. She felt valuable. Precious. Special. As the images of her nightmare slowly began to fade, her body relaxed. She cherished the moment; memorized it. The next time fear paralyzed her, she'd recall this moment.

"You still awake?"

Barely. So close—so exhausted—she didn't think she'd even have the strength to answer. She didn't want to speak; she was safe. Nothing could penetrate this haven—

"I love you", he whispered.

Her body remained still, but her mind was racing. This wasn't supposed to happen! Their relationship was supposed to remain casual. Fun. Emotionless. He didn't mean it—*he couldn't mean it!*

He was just confused.

Yeah.

He felt guilty about what'd happened to her and he was confusing his guilt with *love...* Oh, God, but what if he wasn't?

Olivia remained in his arms, her mind too alert to return to sleep. She stared at the alarm clock, the red illuminated numbers indicating it was nearing five o'clock. Things were getting too serious and she needed to do something about it.

Carefully, she pried herself from Grant's arms and rolled away from him. She needed distance; couldn't bear waking in a few hours with his loving eyes staring into hers.

Quietly, she changed her clothes and tiptoed out of his bedroom. She'd left her toiletries in the bathroom, but she'd worry about that later. Right now, she needed to get as far from him as she could.

Sensing her troubles, Dexter followed her to the front door. "Sorry, boy", she whispered as she knelt down to scratch behind his ears, "Don't take it personal. I've got to get goin'. Be a good boy and go lie down." She stood as Dexter trotted back to his favorite spot on the overstuffed loveseat, his chocolate coat suddenly camouflaged against the brown fabric.

Olivia opened the front door and then glanced over her shoulder one last time. Just a few short hours ago, this had been her safe haven. She was going to miss this place; miss Dexter's greetings, dinners on the deck overlooking the calm Gulf water, lying next to Grant in his bed...

Grant.

Quietly, she closed the door behind her and began the five block trek back home. The sooner she arrived, the sooner she could fall to pieces.

The house was eerily quiet as she dead-bolted the door behind her. For the first time since her attack, she was alone... Images of that frightening night flashed through her mind as her eyes traversed the dark living room. Suppressing the gruesome memories, she willed herself to step forward.

Reaching the familiarity of her childhood bedroom, she knelt down and reached for the black, leather-wrapped scrapbook hidden beneath her antique canopy bed: her "personal portfolio." The corners were beginning to wear, but somehow she couldn't find the strength within herself to replace it.

Opening the portfolio, she smiled at the image staring back at her: her parents. It was the last family portrait taken before their death. Ty was eighteen; she was eight. Her parents looked so happy—little did they all know that less than six months later, everything would forever change.

Turning the page, Olivia skimmed over the newspaper clipping recounting her parents' fatal car accident. They'd gone to dinner in Downtown Atlanta. She remembered it was unusually cold that mid-April evening and the remnants of two days worth of rain blanketed the roads with a slick layer of moisture.

Her father had decided to take the winding back roads instead of the four-lane highway... and so did the drunk driver that hit them. It was a head-on collision. She learned later that her parents had died instantly: one minute they were here, enjoying life, and the next...

Olivia thumbed through the book, each page another significant moment in her life. There were pictures of major milestones like her thirteenth birthday party; photographs of gratifying achievements like her college graduation; mementos from some of her darkest times...

The newspaper clipping from eighteen months ago represented one of those dark times...

One of her photographer friends had set her up on a blind date with a local, well-known dentist. She'd just arrived back into town after traveling to Missouri to photograph the rising flood water. She'd been exhausted—wanted to cancel—but had ultimately decided against it.

His name was Todd Zimmerman.

On the outside he was a very attractive man: tall, dark hair, charcoal eyes, and a perfect smile. She never suspected his good looks disguised a sly sexual predator.

She'd finished her third glass of wine and had excused herself from the table, hoping a wet paper towel on her face and neck would cool her heated skin. She'd just placed the cold compress to her neck when she'd caught a glimpse of Todd standing behind her in the mirror.

He'd covered her mouth, silencing her scream. And then, his free hand began roaming over her body. He'd lifted her skirt, his fingers curling underneath the waistband of her panties, when the door suddenly swung open...

Another man had stumbled in—too drunk to realize he'd entered the women's restroom—but thankfully not too far gone to come to her rescue.

Todd was arrested, charged with sexual assault; three days later, four brave women came forward with similar stories...

The encounter caused her already untrustworthy heart to become more guarded—that is until she'd met Grant.

He loved her.

And that scared her to death. Everyone she'd ever allowed to get that close had left her in some way or fashion: her parents—even Ty. As much as she disliked Cameron, she'd been happy for her brother. He'd sacrificed so much to raise her and he deserved his happiness, too. He'd always invited her home for the holidays, but she'd always declined. He had a wife—a new family—and she wasn't a part of it.

Olivia reached into her nightstand and removed the picture she'd taken of her and Grant on the beach last month. The corners of her mouth tilted upward as she recalled that day.

Grant loved her...

And she was falling for him...

But it was only a matter of time before he'd leave her like all the others had, too. As much as it pained her, she had to walk away first. It was better this way; she gave up on "happily ever after" a long time ago.

CHAPTER 20

Removing his key from the lock, Ty opened the front door and tossed the mail on the small bureau in the foyer. He drifted into the kitchen like a zombie, his body thirsting for caffeine—and lots of it. He paused momentarily as he approached the coffee-maker. *Hmmm, that's odd... It was already on...*

Movement on the patio caught his attention.

Olivia.

Storming through the French doors, he rushed toward her. "What the hell are you doing?" he shouted as he approached.

"What does it look like I'm doing?" she asked as she raised her mug. "It's a beautiful morning to—"

"You know that's not what I meant—you're supposed to be with Grant!"

"You worry too much", she uttered non-chalantly.

Crossing his arms over his chest, his angry eyes bored into hers. *"Really?* You were nearly killed less than two weeks ago—or don't you remember...?

Pulling her knees into her chest, she hugged her legs with her free hand. "Yeah, that's the problem: I *do* remember... Look, I know you're upset, but don't be mad at Grant. I snuck out earlier—he probably doesn't even know—"

"What?" he asked angrily. "How did you get home?"

"Well, I walked."

"Olivia!" Ty sat down across from her and pressed his thumb and index finger against his clenched eyes. After inhaling a gallon of fresh morning air, he finally spoke again. "Listen, I know everything."

"You know everything about *what*...?" she asked confusedly.

"You and Grant—and let me tell ya: *I'm not exactly thrilled about it!*"

"Wait—how'd you?—"

"I figured it out at the hospital when he came to visit you." Leaning his arms on his knees, he inched forward. "I swear to God, Liv, if he hurt you—"

"He didn't", she assured him. "He's been really, really good to me, Ty... If anyone's gonna get hurt, it's gonna be Grant..."

The soft red glow of the safe light temporarily soothed her weary eyes; couldn't say the same about her mind, though. Her brain was so congested, over-crowded with questions she had no answers to.

Was her attacker still lurking in the shadows, ready to pounce again?

Did Grant *really* love her?

Did she have the strength to end their relationship?

Could she pretend she wasn't falling for him, too?

So. Many. Questions...

She didn't want to think about that right now. In fact, she didn't want to think about anything. Switching her mind to its automatic pilot mode, she poured fixer solution into the basin in front of her. The best part of developing her own film?—she could almost do it with her eyes closed, which meant she didn't have to think at all...

Opening the back of her ancient 35mm camera, she removed the film. And that's when she heard it: four loud knocks. "Who is it?" she asked, already knowing who stood on the other side.

"It's me, Grant."

"The door shut behind you?"

"Yeah."

Olivia reached for the knob, unlocked the door, and then retraced her steps back to the counter where she'd been working. She needed to keep her hands busy. The last time he'd visited her darkroom, she'd ended up against the door with her legs wrapped around his waist.

"What the hell do you think you're doing?" he questioned sternly.

Her back still turned, she answered, "What does it look like I'm doing?—I'm developing film."

Bracing his hands on either side of her on the counter, he stood behind her. "You know what I mean. I woke up this morning and panicked when you weren't there. I was about to call the police when Ty called and said you'd walked home earlier. Are you out of your fucking mind?"

"My mind has never been clearer", she lied.

"You could've been hurt!"

"I'm perfectly fine, Grant."

Lowering his head, he released a heavy sigh. "Cut the bullshit, Livvy. I'm not buying it... You don't have to act tough around me."

"I'm not acting", she lied again. She really needed to stop that.

Gripping her arms, he spun her around. "Yes, you are! Look at me..." He watched as her eyes danced around, landing on various objects before hesitantly connecting with his. "You're doing it again", he uttered softly.

"Doing what?"

"Pushing me away! *Why? Why, Livvy...?* Last night, I thought—"

"Last night I had a moment of weakness, but I'm better now. I'm not gonna let this bastard scare me anymore..."

Peeling her focus away from his intense gaze, she lowered her head. What she was about to say was going to be tough, but it had to be done. She needed to do it quickly—like ripping off a band aid—before she lost what little courage she had left.

"Listen, I really appreciate your concern—I really do—but I can take care of myself."

"I know you *can,* but—"

"I need to focus on my work, Grant. I've been ignoring my biggest priority too often lately and... and I can't afford any distractions right now."

"What are you saying?" he asked discon-certedly.

"You should go", she whispered, unable to find her voice.

What the hell? Grant lifted her chin with his fingertips, forcing her to look him in the eye. "So I'm a *distraction?*" Her silence said more than any words she could've spoken. Removing his fingertips from her chin, he wiped his hand down his face. Rage rose within him like searing magma, threatening to explode.

She thought he was a distraction... Like a car alarm whose siren sounded with deafening precision; a hungry mosquito buzzing in her ear... *a Goddamn distraction!*

He needed to get out of this room before he did something else distracting—like confess how much he loved her. "Alright then", he mumbled as he pivoted toward the door.

Olivia watched helplessly as he disappeared from view, leaving her alone.

Alone.

Why couldn't she be brave? Why couldn't she trust his love?—trust her heart?

Because she was terrified of loss. So terrified that she'd deliberately hurt Grant before he had an opportunity to hurt her.

The look on his face when he'd asked if he was a distraction had almost killed her. Almost. She reminded herself that she didn't have a choice. The important people in her life tended not to "stick."

Trusting her heart would only result in its death. Because it was only a matter of time before he'd realize she wasn't the woman she proclaimed to be; she was a fraud.

He was in love with the carefree, picture perfect image she'd cultivated years ago—not the *real* her...

* * * * *

Friday night poker...

Grant was in no mood to play, but Olivia had been avoiding him all week. He wasn't confident he'd win, but he was confident he'd get an opportunity to see her, talk to her. And that was worth any amount of money he'd lose in the process.

After ringing the doorbell, he shoved his hands in his front pockets and drew in a deep breath. As soon as the door opened, he stepped inside, his eyes scanning the room for her presence.

"Eager to lose your money tonight, are you?" Randall asked as he closed the door behind them.

"Yeah, something like that."

"Well, good—I owe a buddy of mine a boat load of cash. Taking yours will be the easiest part-time gig I've ever had!"

Most of the guys and their significant others had already arrived, the living room cluttered with warm bodies immersed in meaningless conversation. An eruption of laughter echoed from the kitchen. And that's when he saw her. She was surrounded by several of the wives, talking, laughing; looking as though she didn't have a care in the world...

That's right, Womack, she looks like a woman with no more distractions...

He'd told himself he wouldn't ambush her—at least not at first. Apparently his body didn't get the memo; before he became conscious of it, he was on the move, his body on a direct collision course with the woman he loved.

"Hey ladies", he announced as he approached. The handful of women all greeted him in unison as he turned toward Olivia. "How are you doing?"

Revealing a smile that didn't quite reach her eyes, she replied, "I've been great."

"Good. I'm... I'm really glad to hear that..."

There was an awkward silence as the crowd of females gawked at the spectacle before them. His feelings for this woman were clearly written all over his face and for the first time in his life, he didn't care.

"You know what?" Lana Phillips interjected. "I left my phone in the car. I think I'd better go get it."

"Yeah, I think I left my drink out on the patio", Tonya woods remarked as she strolled toward the French doors.

"Wait up—I'll go with you."

"Me, too", announced Jenny Carson.

Suddenly, it was just the two of them.

"I thought they'd never leave", he said as he revealed a mischievous grin. Olivia smiled too—not the fake smile she'd pasted earlier—but a real, *genuine* smile that brightened her delicate features and warmed his heart.

His eyes perused her body. She was wearing a plum-colored blouse that complimented her soft tanned skin; a slim pair of dark denim jeans that emphasized her delectable curves and a pair of black suede stilettos. Her hair was set in soft voluminous curls, reminding him of how it appeared the night she'd transformed into a sexy referee.

And those lips...

Plump. Supple. Irresistible.

They were layered with a shiny peach gloss and he wondered if they tasted as delicious as they appeared...

*Of course they did. That was a stupid fucking
question, Womack.*

Yeah, it was.

"You look beautiful", he finally managed to say.

"Thank you."

Grant leaned his shoulder against the refrigerator and shoved his hands back into his pockets
before he did something really stupid: reach for her.
"I was... hoping that maybe we could talk later, you
know? After everyone leaves? I... really miss you,
Livvy."

Olivia stared into his mesmerizing eyes, the
radiant blue hue unable to camouflage the anguish
he was experiencing.

Nor the love.

The doorbell rang, jolting her back to reality. "I
can't, Grant. I'm sorry, but I've already made plans."
Plans to push you even further away...

"Oh—"

"—Hey Olivia, you ready?"

Grant glanced over his shoulder... Jarrod
James stood behind him, his eyes hungry for a taste
of *his* Livvy.

"Yeah, let me just grab my purse." Olivia
reached behind her on the counter for her black
leather clutch and when she turned around, the
betrayal on Grant's face nearly suffocated her.

Was this some kind of a sick joke? He was a
"distraction", but Jarrod wasn't? Grant tilted his head
back toward Jarrod. "What's this all about?" He inquired through clenched teeth.

"Dinner, Grant—I'm hungry..." Olivia placed
her free hand on his forearm and squeezed. "I'll see
you later, okay?"

* * * * *

Glancing over her shoulder, Olivia took in the view from their table along the deck. The moon's reflection glistened in the calm Gulf and the rhythmic cadence of gentle waves colliding against the wood pilings below lulled her. She allowed her mind to settle in a brief reverie: the night everything changed.

Two months earlier, she'd sat across from Grant at this very table on their first date, unaware that their casual intentions would evolve into something so authentic. So rare. Closing her eyes, she recalled that evening: dinner, the Ferris wheel ride, their kiss...

"You alright?" Jarrod asked kindheartedly. "You haven't said much since we sat down."

Olivia turned her attention back to Jarrod. Under different circumstances, the attractive blonde man sitting to her right would've easily absorbed her attention. But somehow, no matter how hard she tried, she couldn't forget about Grant.

She was being unfair—she knew; there were plenty of single women who'd happily trade places with her right now. Plenty of women who'd give anything for Jarrod to aim his dark gaze in their direction.

"I'm sorry", she uttered as she smiled. "I guess I just got lost in the beautiful view."

"It is a beautiful view—although I'm not sure if we're referring to the same scenery", he said as he gave her a wink.

Olivia nervously tucked her hair behind her ear and attempted to steer the conversation toward a safer topic. "How long have you been a firefighter?"

"About three years", Jarrod replied.

"And what did you do before that?" Olivia asked before she took a sip of wine.

"Played football."

Olivia tilted her head. "Let me guess: quarter-back?"

Jarrod smiled. "You're good—how'd you know?"

"I don't know", she said as she shrugged her shoulders, "you just look the part, I guess. You have a lot in common with Randall, ya know; he was our quarterback in high school and then went on to play at the local community college."

She observed him for a few moments. His eyes seemed to glaze over as though he were reliving one of his fondest memories, and then his brows furrowed. "So you stopped playing after graduation?"

Jarrod shrugged his shoulders. "Injured my shoulder at the start of my senior year in college. By the time it healed, no one was interested in taking a chance on me."

She could almost feel disappointment radiant off him in waves. Instinctively, she reached out and grabbed his hand. "I'm really sorry, Jarrod."

Shrugging his shoulder again, he stroked the stubble along his jaw with his free hand. "Ah, it's alright. Guess it just wasn't meant to be…"

The waitress suddenly appeared, gently placing their meals in front of them. And after refilling their water glasses and handing Jarrod another beer, she disappeared inside.

"Wow! This looks delicious!" she acknowledged as she removed her hand from his grip.

"Trust me, it is", he shared. "Is this your first

time here?"

"Um... no. No, I've been here before. Once..."

With Grant... our first date...

"Alright, now it's my turn to ask twenty questions", he informed her as he placed his beer back on the table.

"Okay, I guess that's only fair. What do you wanna know?"

"Everything..."

Groaning, Olivia slowly reached for the phone. "Hello?"

"You up?" Grant asked.

"Well, I am now—"

"—Good. Get dressed; I'll be there in fifteen minutes to pick you up. We're having breakfast."

Olivia sighed. "Grant, can I take a rain check?" she asked as she massaged her temple with her free hand.

"No. Now you have fourteen minutes. I'll see you then."

She really didn't need this right now. What she needed to do was turn over and go back to bed! She'd taken a dose of Benadryl after she'd returned from dinner with Jarrod last night, hoping it would knock her out so she'd sleep. It worked—maybe a little too well. She felt groggy, her mind clouded in a drowsy fog. But she knew Grant; he wasn't going to take "no" for an answer.

And after what she did to him last night, she didn't exactly blame him.

Every time she closed her eyes, she saw the look of bewilderment on his face when he realized she was going to dinner with Jarrod. She hated herself for doing that.

Hated that she'd had to.

Rising from bed, she quickly dressed in a black velour jogging suit, brushed her teeth and pulled her long hair back into a loose ponytail. As promised, he arrived in exactly fourteen minutes.

He'd taken her back to his beach house, a dozen doughnuts from Anderson's Bakery awaiting them on the back patio. Sitting next to him, absorbing the luminous rays of the rising sun, revived her.

Her eyes quickly roamed over the picturesque landscape, and then they became transfixed on the man beside her. His jaw was clenched tight: an attempt to simmer his growing temper. She kept waiting for him to lose it, to slam his fist against the table and yell. But he didn't.

Instead, he shocked her by keeping the aura light and easy—as though last night had never happened. There was no mention of Jarrod; no mention of her odd behavior.

She was sharing some of her fondest memories of Ty bringing home doughnuts on his way home from shift when she was a little girl, when Grant inched forward toward her. Raising his hand to her face, his thumb brushed against the corner of her mouth. She paused in mid-sentence as he brought his thumb to his lips.

"Mmmm, lemon cream... That's good. I'll have to get that next time."

Oh, God! Stay strong—stand your ground!

"Thanks for breakfast. Can't think of a better way to start the day than with fresh doughnuts and coffee.

Makes me miss home."

"Home?"

"New Orleans", she said as she smiled. "The first thing I'm gonna do when I get back is head to Café Du Monde and order myself a chicory coffee and *two* beignets!" She said as she gestured with her fingers.

She watched as he drew in a deep breath and slowly exhaled through his mouth. "Um, I'm should probably get back to the house; I've got a lot of work to do in the darkroom today."

Grant searched her face. She was holding back.

But *why?*

He wanted to push until she revealed the reasons behind her sudden about-face, wanted to shake her until the walls she'd erected crumbled to the ground. But what good would that do? She'd only shove him further away and he refused to let that happen. He loved her. If she needed space, he'd give it to her.

But he refused to give up.

He'd managed to stay in control until he pulled into the driveway of her home, and then his restraint failed him. Shoving his truck into park, he leaned over the console and palmed the side of her face, drawing her in for a kiss.

The moment she felt his lips against her mouth, her will dissolved. His kiss comforted, quieting her doubts, easing her fears. She gave in at first, reacquainting her tongue with his taste. Her hands roamed over his hard chest, past his broad shoulders, before finally fisting in his hair. She still wanted him—all of him—for the rest of her life. She wanted to cling to this man for all of eternity.

She wanted what she couldn't have...

She tasted like coffee, fresh citrus, and desire. He wanted to reel her back in, needed her to remember how incredible they were together. He put everything he had into their kiss, hoping to communicate how important she'd become in his life. And how necessary she was to his existence.

A soft needy moan escaped from the back of her throat as she surrendered. He savored the sound as it reverberated through his body. And as if suddenly realizing that the sensual sigh had come from her, she stiffened in his arms and tried to pull away.

"Grant—"

He allowed her to unseal their mouths, but he didn't release her completely. Resting his forehead against hers, he asked the questions that'd been plaguing him for days. "Damn it, Livvy, what the hell is going on? Why are you so determined to shove me away?"

"I'm not pushing you away—"

Releasing her, he leaned back in the driver's seat and after expelling a puff of air from his lungs, he pinched the bridge of his nose and closed his eyes. His jaw was clenched tightly, so much so that he feared his teeth would shatter. "So going on a date with Jarrod isn't pushing me away?"

"It was *just* dinner—"

"—It was a date..." With the back of his head still resting on the seat, he turned his head toward her. "When did you decide we were gonna start seeing other people?"

Olivia wrapped her arms around her body, enveloping herself in as much comfort as she could conjure up. "Since when did you decide that we were exclusive?" she countered.

"Gee, Livvy, I don't know—I guess it was right before you were attacked when you practically begged me to fuck you! That sound about right?" he asked angrily. "You set the pace, remember?"

Moisture stung the back of her eyes, but she refused to reveal how deeply his words and surly tone affected her. Lowering her head, she clenched them shut. "I'm... I'm sorry you misunderstood, Grant. You've been a really good friend to me and—"

"—Friend?" he interjected. "Is that all I am to you?—just a friend?"

God, no! You're so much more—you're everything...

Could she do this? Could she really do this? — walk away from this man with no regrets?

You have no choice. "I'm so sorry, Grant. I honestly never meant to hurt you."

"Yeah", he uttered softly.

It was a tragedy to walk away from what they'd shared, but it would be far worse months from now when he'd likely leave her.

Olivia opened the door to his truck and forced herself to take one final look at the man she wanted, but couldn't have. She'd dealt the final blow; mauled his heart. She needed to get to her room quickly; the levee was moments away from bursting and gravity would soon take hold of her tears.

A series of soft knocks temporarily suspended the implosion of self-pity and guilt she'd suffered since she'd exited Grant's truck earlier that morning. Olivia wiped at her eyes with her fingertips, expunging the vertical path of her tears, and then quickly shoved her personal portfolio underneath her pillow.

"Come in."

Ty lazily opened the door. "Hey squirt", he greeted as he joined her on the edge of the bed.

"Hey", she answered softly.

Leaning forward, he stared straight ahead. There was no doubt about it: she'd been crying. Sure, she'd wiped her tears before he entered, but she couldn't hide the red tint of her eyes or the swollen shadowy skin surrounding them.

The discovery pummeled his heart. He couldn't remember her ever crying—not even when their parents had died. She'd always kept her emotions hidden from view, under lock and key; their sudden liberation was monumental.

"Last night with Jarrod... that was a little... *unexpected.*"

"Jesus, Joseph and Mary, you sound just like Grant! It was *just dinner,* okay?"

"Okay... Can I ask you one more question, though? Why are you crying? Did Grant hurt you?—is that it? Were you using Jarrod for revenge?"

"That's more than one question", she teased.

"Alright, let's start with the first one then..."

Olivia covered her mouth with one of her hands, desperately trying to withhold the despair threatening to flee. Heavy tears rained down her cheeks as her fortitude faltered. "No. Grant's been... he's been amazing. He didn't hurt me, Ty—*I hurt him...*"

"Wow, that's definitely a first! Don't think anyone's done that before. He's usually the heartbreaker."

"Yeah", she whispered. Wiping at her eyes again, she stood from the bed. "What's done is done... If you need me, I'll be in my darkroom."

Ty wiped his hand down his face as she drifted toward the door. Damn it, he didn't know which was worse: thinking that she never cried or witnessing it firsthand.

The latter—most definitely the latter!

Glancing around the room, his eyes landed on a dark object wedged underneath her pillow: her personal portfolio. He hadn't seen it in years. The leather covering was worn around the edges, indicating it'd gotten a lot of use over the years.

Opening it was the closest thing to time travel he'd ever experienced. Suddenly, he was propelled back in time, eighteen years ago. He'd never forget that dreaded phone call, or the brave face Olivia had exhibited when he'd arrived hours later. That was the first pivotal moment in her young life, but it certainly wasn't the last.

As he thumbed through the pages, he relived each moment. Not all were bad—there were good moments, too. Her thirteenth birthday: he'd survived a slumber party with eight of her childhood friends—and the shaving cream fight that materialized at the stroke of midnight. Her senior year: crowned Miss Winterfest. Early 2008: her first cover at Adversity Magazine...

Each moment—good and bad—molded her into the person she was today. She was a survivor, a crusader. Sometimes he envied her bravery, her courage. Hell, his wife had left him with a Dear John letter and a broken heart months ago; divorce papers arrived back in October and he still lacked the strength to sign on the dotted line.

Why?

Because he wasn't brave—not like Olivia. He'd been in denial for so long he'd become complacent with his heartache, idle—

"Holy shit", he mumbled as he turned to the last page. Olivia's feelings for Grant were far more serious than she'd let on and the discovery of this picture was proof.

CHAPTER 21

"Say somethin' ", Olivia prodded. She stared at her best friend for several moments, Kendall's wide eyes and slack jaw indicating she'd taken her by surprise. But the real clincher: she'd rendered Kendall speechless. That was certainly a first.

"Kendall...? Are you still with me?"

"I'm your best friend", she began.

"Yes."

"And you know I love you to pieces."

"Uh-huh."

"And you know that I will always tell you the truth—no matter how awful it may be."

"Yes, I'm—"

"What kind of dope have you been smokin'? Grant Womack is head-over-heels in love with you! Get your head out of your ass so you can see what's right in front of you!—or in this case", she whispered as she cupped her hands around her mouth, "what's behind you."

Olivia glanced over her shoulder as Grant

trekked toward the pool tables along the back wall of the saloon. It didn't appear as though he'd noticed her. At least that's what she attempted to convince herself. It hurt far too much to think he'd purposely avoided her.

Yeah, like you've managed to do countless times.

Turning around, she shrugged her shoulders. "I have no control over his feelings, but I do have control over mine. I don't wanna lead him on. He's a good guy; soon he'll realize I did us both a huge favor."

"This must be my lucky day", Jarrod said as he approached the varnished wood bar. "The two prettiest females in town, sitting together. Santa must've thought I was a good boy this year!"

"Flattering will get you everywhere, Jarrod", Kendall affirmed.

"So will a drink. How 'bout it?—what can I get you ladies?"

"Nothing for me", Kendall announced as she finished the last of her gin and tonic. "I have to be at the pharmacy early in the morning."

"Okay—what about you, Olivia...?"

Torture: that's what this was, Grant acknowledged. Mutilate him, waterboard him—hell, hook his ass up to a car battery and zap him—anything was better than this. He'd noticed Olivia the moment he'd arrived. She'd been sitting at the bar with Kendall, recounting her date with Jarrod no doubt. He ignored the way she looked in her faded jeans; ignored how she'd tied her flannel shirt in a knot at her narrow waist; ignored how she pursed her plump lips together when she took a pull from her imported beer.

Yeah, you ignored her alright...

Okay, so maybe his eyes revisited the bar from time to time. Was that so terrible?

No, at least not at first. It only became a real problem when Jarrod arrived. He'd turned on that charismatic charm and the next thing Grant knew, Kendall was heading out the door, leaving the town's hottest new couple alone for a second date!

"Alright, Womack, how much are we wagering this round?" Randall asked as he placed the billiard balls inside the triangle on the pool table.

"Forty."

"Forty? C'mon, man—I've got debts to pay! Make it seventy-five and I'll let you break."

"Debts to pay?—to who?" he asked as he turned his attention back to Randall. "You inherited your house and your truck's been paid-off for months."

"It's nothing serious—I just owe a buddy of mine some cash."

Grant picked up the small cube of chalk and twisted it back and forth over the tip of his cue stick and then placed it on the side of the billiard table. "You're not in any kind of trouble, are you?"

"No—but you're 'bout to be if you don't hurry up with the break shot", Randall teased.

Olivia closed one of her eyes and focused on the dartboard in front of her. It didn't help; she still saw two of them.

"Anyone ever tell you how cute you look when you're trying to concentrate?" Jarrod asked.

"Is that your subtle way of distracting me? The

board's a little fuzzy, but I can still make it out!"

Jarrod shook his head and smiled. "Here, let me help", he offered as he slid off the wooden stool.

"Does it look like I need help?" She asked as she placed her hands on her hips.

"Do you really want me to answer that...?"

"Okay", she conceded, "point taken." She could feel the warmth of his body as he approached from behind. An odd zing zipped up her spine as one of his hands wrapped around her midsection, tugging her closer. His other hand assisted her in launching the dart.

"Hey, man, you gonna shoot?—or are you gonna stand there and eye Olivia all night?" Randall inquired. "I mean—don't get me wrong—I'd much rather spend the night lookin' at her than you. But—"

"Sorry, bro."

"Do me a favor: picture Jarrod's face on the cue ball and smack the shit out of it so I can hurry up and collect my winnings."

Grant walked around the edge of the pool table and got into position for his next shot. He eased the stick over his thumb back and forth several times to get the feel of it, when suddenly movement up ahead at the dartboard snagged his undivided attention.

The dart struck against the board with a heavy thud. She may have been seeing double, but both images indicated that she'd just missed the bull's eye by a fraction. Jarrod tightened his grip as he buried his face in the crook of her neck. Another strange sensation came over her, and it wasn't until he spoke again that she recognized why.

"Good shot, Blondie!" Jarrod felt the overly intoxicated beauty clutched in his arms petrify.

Where do you think you're going, Blondie?

I sure am sorry 'bout all this, Blondie. Things would've turned out much better for you if you'd only cooperated.

Why don't you make yourself useful: pose that pretty lil' ass in front of the camera instead of sneaking around, taking pictures of me. Stay out of my way or next time, things might not turn out so well for you...

Oh. My. God.

"What's the matter, Olivia?" Jarrod whispered against her ear. "You act like you just saw a ghost."

She forced herself to turn her head toward him. She needed to gage his reaction. It wasn't as if she were the only blonde in town; maybe his choice of words had been merely coincidental. "Or maybe an arsonist..."

Something wasn't right—something didn't feel right. Grant shoved the tip of his stick against the cue ball. After missing his target, he took a seat on the wood stool along the back wall and watched helplessly as Jarrod wrapped his arms around Olivia and buried his face in the crook of her neck.

Rage and fury saturated his dark eyes and that's when she knew. "Damn it, it was *you*", she mumbled.

"Careful, Blondie, I don't want to see you get hurt again."

* * * * *

They weren't moving—they were just standing there. Grant took another pull from his beer.

Why the hell was he still here? He should've left the moment he realized Olivia was sitting at the bar.

What was he trying to prove?—that he was unfazed by her sudden interest in Jarrod?—that he no longer cared what she did or who she did it with?

If that's what he was trying to do, he was failing miserably.

Gripping the bottle, he raised it to his lips again—and then froze...

Jarrod couldn't believe he'd slipped and called her "Blondie". It'd rolled off his tongue with such ease. He was hoping that she didn't remember, but the sudden rigidness of her body against his and the unmistakable terror in her big green eyes said otherwise.

Now, he had to think fast—before she screamed and exposed his identity to everyone in the crowded saloon. "Let's take a walk", he said as he gripped her arm above her elbow. "You look like you could use some fresh air."

"No, I—"

He strengthened his grip and lowered his voice for emphasis. "It's not up for discussion, Olivia. Either you do as I ask, or someone you really care about will suffer. Let's go—*now.*"

She didn't know where he was taking her or what he'd do with her once they arrived at their destination, but she did know one thing: she wasn't going to allow him to hurt anyone she cared about.

Olivia had turned her head toward Jarrod. At first, Grant thought he was about to witness a kiss, but then he caught a glimpse of her expression as her eyes traveled up the contours of Jarrod's face: recognition and... *unadulterated fear.*

Jarrod leaned in, whispered something in her ear, and then gripped her arm just above her elbow.

"Your shot, bro", Randall announced.

Pivoting, the town's hottest new couple headed back toward the bar. Jarrod reached into his pocket and tossed a few bills toward the bartender.

"You spacing out on me again? I said it was your shot."

Something wasn't right. His gut told him they weren't planning a leisurely stroll down the boardwalk. Rising from the stool, Grant reached into his wallet and placed a one-hundred dollar bill on the pool table.

"Listen, Randall, I'm gonna have to forfeit this round. Something's come up."

"Ah, man—I don't have change for a one-hundred dollar—"

Grant slapped him on the back of the shoulder and gave it a squeeze. "Don't worry 'bout it—consider it my forfeiting fee."

Grant rushed toward the front door and stumbled into the brisk dark night. The moon was hidden behind a thick blanket of clouds. He looked left and then right. "Damn it", he mumbled. There was no sign of them anywhere.

* * * * *

Jarrod had a death grip on her arm. His long stride was no match for her small five foot, four inch frame; he'd practically dragged her alongside him. "Listen, Jarrod, it's been fun—really—but it's been a long day. I think I'm gonna call it a night."

The laughter that escaped him was somber and evil-like. Where was the kind, funny, interesting man that'd taken her to dinner several days earlier? She wondered.

"Like hell you are", he said as he steered her toward the wood pilings beneath the pier.

"C'mon, Jarrod—it's over. I know who you are and soon, everyone else will, too."

In one swift motion, he turned her around and then shoved her body back against the wood piling, sandwiching her between his body and the solid structure. "Now that's where you're wrong. You see, you're not gonna be around to tell anyone about what I've done."

"Damn it, Jarrod—what're you gonna do?—kill me?" she asked breathlessly.

Jarrod caressed her cheek with the back of his hand. "I may be a lot of things, sweetheart, but I'm not a murderer. I know you may not believe this, but I never meant to hurt you—"

"You left me lying in a puddle of my own blood, Jarrod."

"I know", he admitted softly as he closed his eyes. "That's not how it was supposed to happen. I never wanted to hurt you, but you kept fighting me." His eyes opened. "I had no choice."

"And now...?" she inquired.

"Now, you have to leave town", he informed her, "tonight. You're gonna lose contact with everyone on this island: your brother, Kendall and especially Womack... Indefinitely."

"And what happens if I don't?"

"Oh, you will. You see"—he began as one of his fingertips traced an invisible line down her right cheek—"I'm real good at planting evidence. And wouldn't it be a shame to find out that your boyfriend's been setting the town ablaze in order to collect some much-needed overtime to renovate his beloved beach house..."

"You wouldn't."

"To save my ass from going to jail?—I most certainly would..."

Grant had been searching along the pier for several minutes when he suddenly came to a halt. Olivia's expression at the saloon was a familiar one: it was the same alarm and anxiety he'd observed during her nightmare last week when she'd stayed with him...

"Holy shit", he mumbled. *Jarrod was the arsonist!*

Panicked, he removed his phone from his front pocket and dialed 911. And when the call had been made, he hurried down the stairs that led to the beach. He just prayed he hadn't realized Jarrod's identity too late.

"So this was all about *money?*" she asked incredulously.

"It's what makes the world go round..."

At that moment, his hard expression softened. And she was finally able to detect that Jarrod was afraid, too.

"I have gambling debts to settle. I owe a lot of money to a very scary man—scarier than me", he admitted.

"If it's money you need, I'll give it to you... I have a trust fund—you can have it—all of it! Please, Jarrod, don't make me walk away from my family!" Tears were stinging the back of her eyes. She didn't want to release them—didn't want to reveal any outward signs of weakness—but wasn't able to hold back.

"I have to", he uttered softly.

"No, Jarrod. I won't tell another soul—you have my word! Please, don't make me do this!"

Jarrod palmed the sides of her face; took in her beauty. Olivia had captivated him from the moment he'd laid eyes on her. Just then, the clouds shifted, revealing the luminous half moon. It was then that he saw her tears, saw the fear in her eyes, comprehended the brutality of what he was asking.

"As much as I want to believe you, Olivia, I can't take the risk. I know—" He paused for a moment: a crescendo of sirens. "Fuck! How did you do that?"

"What, Jarrod?—I didn't do anything, I swear!" she sobbed.

"I'm sorry, Blondie. I'm so sorry", he uttered softly as he pressed his lips against hers.

The police sirens had caught her by surprise—and so had the kiss. And then as he pulled away, he looked into her eyes and she saw it: fear, panic, regret. He was moments away from captivity, moments away from *his* worst nightmare.

Kissing Olivia was heavenly. He was finally able to taste her, to commit it to memory. Her soft, plump lips felt amazing pressed against his. For as long as he lived, he would remember this.

The sirens were getting louder: it was now or never...

Reluctantly, he pulled away and tightened his grip on her face. God, he didn't want to do this, but he had no choice. He drove her head back against the wood piling and winced when he heard her skull strike against the solid structure. And then without a backward glance, he sprinted...

A piercing scream had Grant racing toward the pilings underneath the boardwalk. It seemed as though he was running in place—which was completely absurd; his feet were pounding the powdery sand so swiftly, he was convinced he could probably dash across the calm Gulf water and remain afloat.

Moments later, he saw her: hovering above the sand on all fours.

"Livvy!" he called out as he collapsed onto his knees beside her. The back of her head glistened against the faint moonlight as blood saturated her honey-blonde hair. "Jesus, Livvy, what the hell did he do to you?"

Olivia gripped his shirt as he assisted her upright. "*Grant?*" she asked confusedly.

God, she looked pale—even in the dim moonlight, he could see: the color had drained from her angelic face. "I'm right here, baby."

"My...my head hurts", she uttered, just above a whisper.

"Did Jarrod do this to you?" He watched as Olivia closed her eyes and nodded her head. *Damn it!* If only he'd listened to his gut sooner. He could have prevented this; could've protected her.

"It was Jarrod James!" Grant shouted as the town's three deputies on duty raced toward them.

"Any idea which way he went?" one of them asked as they approached.

"Livvy", Grant uttered as he palmed the sides of her face, "did you see which way he went?"

Olivia nodded cautiously and pointed down the beach toward the marina. The deputies sprinted away from them with their weapons drawn. She watched until their black uniforms disappeared into the dark night. And then she turned her attention to Grant.

Her heart skipped a beat at the sight of him. And as if her body sensed the safety of his arms, her eyes closed and serenity prevailed.

CHAPTER 22

Grant exited the gift shop and boarded the elevator with a large bouquet of pale pink roses in hand. Reluctantly, he'd left the hospital last night at the urging of Olivia's nurse. Olivia was only allowed one overnight guest, and he wasn't about to ask Ty to forfeit his privileges. He'd been told that visiting hours would resume at nine o'clock sharp the following morning and as he glanced at his watch, he acknowledged he was right on time.

The elevator opened to the second floor and Grant pointed his feet toward the extended corridor that led to Olivia's room. He thought back to the last time he'd been here, the morning after her first attack. He hadn't known what to expect then—knew only that she'd been badly injured.

He'd been reeling from the incredible evening he'd had with her when Ty had phoned him that morning. Back then, he didn't have a face to direct his anger toward; now he did: *Jarrod fucking James!*

Why hadn't he put two and two together

sooner? It made perfect sense now: James' multiple absences from poker night, his frequent trips to the dog track just outside of Pensacola, his prompt arrival to every fire—and let's not forget—his fascination with Olivia.

Jarrod had torched thousands of dollars worth of private property and had nearly killed Olivia in the process...

Over gambling debts.

Grant shook his head as the realization sunk in. He would have gladly loaned the money to Jarrod had he known how desperate he was to get his hands on it.

Luckily, Jarrod had been apprehended last night; charged with seven counts of arson and two counts of aggravated battery.

Sedating his lungs with a gallon of oxygen, Grant nudged the door to Olivia's room open...

The room was empty and from the looks of it, it had been for some time.

Retracing his steps, he moved toward the nurses' station and caught the attention of a kind, elderly R.N. "Excuse me, has Olivia Everitt been moved? I just went to the room she was in last night, but it was empty."

"The cute lil' blonde with that nasty gash on the back of her head?" she questioned.

"That's the one."

"She checked herself out against Dr. Conrad's orders—"

"—When?"

"Oh, I don't know—three—maybe four hours ago."

* * * * *

A peculiar phenomenon had washed over him; after meandering through the hospital parking lot in search of his truck, he'd had what could only be described as an "out-of-body experience." He vaguely remembered the drive to Ty and Olivia's. It was almost like he was hovering above his body, like his mind was completely detached from his physical self. He couldn't say for certain which route he'd taken or how long he'd been on the road. The only thing he knew for sure was that he was sitting behind the wheel of his oversized Ford pick-up, idling in Ty and Olivia's driveway.

After exiting his truck, he drifted toward the front door and pounded on the dense wood with his fist.

"What the hell's going on?" he demanded as Ty answered the door. "I just left the hospital and they said she checked herself out!"

"Good morning to you, too, bro", he uttered sarcastically. "Have a seat; we need to talk."

Ah, hell, this couldn't be good, Grant acknowledged. He knew Ty wasn't happy about his relationship with Olivia. He expected Ty's anger and disappointment: it wasn't exactly breaking news that his best friend was furious at him for secretly dating his little sister. But what he soon realized, after situating himself on the red leather sofa, was that Ty's anger and disappointment was no longer directed at him: it was now focused on Olivia.

"So, you just left the hospital, huh?" Ty asked nonchalantly as he blew into his steaming coffee mug.

"Yeah—what the hell's going on? Where is she?" Grant demanded.

"Gone."

"Gone?—what do you mean*?"*

"Liv got a call just after midnight from one of her photographer friends. Apparently, there was a ski lift collapse at a resort in Northern New Hampshire. She... jumped at the chance to photograph it."

"She's in no condition to travel—why didn't you try to stop her?"

Ty took a sip of coffee and nearly choked as he stifled a laugh. "Are you *serious?* You know Liv—she doesn't take orders very well; 'bout the only way I could've made her stay was have the hospital staff strap her to her bed!"

Grant leaned forward, resting his elbows on his lap. Ty was right. But that didn't make the news of her sudden disappearance any easier. "Alright, so when will she be back?"

"Yeah, that's the thing—I'm not really sure when or *if* she's planning on coming back."

"Cut the bullshit, bro—what do you mean *if?"*

Ty exhaled a puff of air and set his coffee mug on the adjacent glass end table. "Before she left, she asked me to visit her in New Orleans for New Year's... January second is her birthday..."

Grant slid the palm of his hand down the contours of his face, but his frustration still remained. "No offense", he uttered softly, "but your sister drives me fucking crazy sometimes."

"None taken."

"I just don't get it. Why would she just up and leave like that?—without even saying goodbye?"

Rising from his seat, Ty sauntered toward the bar and reached for Olivia's portfolio. "She left in such a hurry, she forgot this. I think you'll find your answer in here", he clarified as he gently tossed it toward Grant.

"What's this?—her diary or somethin'?" Grant questioned.

"Well, sort of: she calls it her *personal portfolio*. Take a look."

Opening the album, Grant stared at an all-American family: The Everitt's. The beautiful little girl sitting on her father's lap, gazing into the camera without a care in the world...

Turning the page, he came upon two newspaper clippings: one that depicted the tragic accident that ended the lives of Olivia's parents, and the obituary that'd reduced their lives to a tiny paragraph.

He continued through the book, skimming over various achievements, milestones, and significant moments from her past. It intrigued him that a child who'd lost her parents could rebound and grow into such a fascinating young woman. But then again, that was Olivia: strong willed, tenacious, courageous. And oh-so beautiful.

Turning the page, he stumbled upon a newspaper article from *The New Orleans Tribune,* dated July of last year:

Local Respected Dentist Refused to Smile in Scandalous Mug Shot.

"What's this?" he questioned as he gestured toward the article.

"Remember when I took some time off last year to visit Liv in New Orleans?" Ty asked as he reached for his forgotten coffee mug.

"Yeah—Fourth of July, right?"

Ty settled in the red leather club chair wedged in the corner of the room and took a sip of his now tepid coffee. "Yeah, it was. But I wasn't in town to watch the city's fireworks display... Liv needed me."

"She'd gone on this blind date with a well-known dentist: well-known for his talent as well as his good looks. Anyhow, the guy was a real Casanova: took her to a classy French Quarter restaurant; ordered a bottle of expensive red wine; said all the right things..."

Shifting a bit in his seat, Ty went on. "She realized she'd probably had too much to drink. She excused herself from the table and went to the ladies room, hoping that a wet paper towel on her face and neck would sober her up a bit... He... followed her into the restroom and snuck up behind her. And then—"

"He didn't—"

"No", Ty confirmed, "He didn't get the chance, thank God. Some drunk guy stumbled into the wrong bathroom and interrupted the bastard... The dentist was arrested that evening and several days after the news became public, four other women came forward with similar stories..."

Grant sat motionless for several moments as the details from yet another tragic event in Olivia's life sunk in. How much hardship could a person endure before they broke in two?

"Liv built a wall after that. She was heavily guarded before that night, but after...?" Ty shook his head. "Sometimes I wondered if she'd ever allow anyone to get close to her again... Then she met you."

"Me?" Grant asked incredulously.

"Yeah", Ty answered on a sigh, "turn the page."

Gently sliding his fingertips beneath the upper right-hand corner of the thick cardstock, he turned the page, smiling at one of his fondest memories: chasing after Olivia on the beach earlier last month. He hadn't noticed the first time she'd shown him this picture, but he clearly saw it now: pure felicity.

At that moment in time, her mind was free; free from the memories that'd haunted her; unshackled from the weight of her burdens; content.

"I figured the two of you were just hangin' out—messin' around. I had no idea how serious it was... She only adds the most significant things to this album—the good and the bad—and when I saw this picture, I knew."

"Knew what?" Grant inquired.

"She's in love with you."

Grant closed the portfolio and placed it on the couch beside him. Resting his elbows on his lap, he brought his hands to his face and tented his fingertips together into a point. "Don't be ridiculous—she doesn't love me. She fucking left without so much as a goodbye and apparently has no intention of coming back!"

"Have you heard a damn thing I just said?" Ty asked as he rose from his chair. "She loves you and that scares the piss out of her because every person she's ever cared about has abandoned her in some way or fashion—*me included!* The wittiness and tough-girl exterior are nothing more than a defense mechanism: a façade. Because truthfully, inside, she's still that vulnerable and terrified nine year old little girl I picked up eighteen years ago..."

Running his fingers through his hair, Grant

expelled a puff of air from his lungs before meeting Ty's curious gaze. "So what am I supposed to do now?"

Ty shrugged his shoulders. "Depends—do you love her?"

"More than anything", he uttered softly.

Ty smiled in spite of himself. It was clear how Olivia felt about Grant, and after talking with his best friend, Ty was convinced that Grant felt the same way for her. Although he was still upset that they'd gone behind his back, he couldn't fault the guy for loving her. And he certainly couldn't allow her stubbornness to stand in the way of her long-awaited fairytale ending.

"Here's whatcha do—I have a plan..."

CHAPTER 23

It'd been two days since Olivia had come home to New Orleans; two days since her friends had practically hauled her to the French Quarter to celebrate the end of one year and the beginning of the next.

She'd been standing in front of Jackson's Square, surrounded by thousands of tourists and locals. And the irony of the situation: she'd never felt more alone. She'd managed to make it all the way 'til ten-thirty that evening, and then lied to her friends about not feeling well. Thirty minutes later, a taxi had dropped her off in front of the guest house she rented in the Garden District.

She'd missed the colorful firework display over the mighty Mississippi River; had instead watched the ball drop from Times Square on TV. Alone.

Completely alone.

She was so afraid—petrified—of love. Allowing herself to be happy could only result in disaster—always had—probably always would. She had accepted it a long time ago; had conceded that she'd never experience "happily ever after." And the funny thing was: she'd been *okay* with it.

Until Grant.

Now she understood what she was missing out on—what she was depriving herself of...

Grant deserved better. He deserved the kind of woman who could open up and give all of herself to him. He deserved the kind of warmth and contentment she wasn't capable of giving.

Her insides were contorted like a Cirque Du Soleil performer. God, she missed him. Missed the sound of his laughter; the intoxicating masculine scent of his skin; the intensity of his ice-blue eyes when they were focused on her...

But this was for the best. Better to endure the unbearable heartache now; there was no need to postpone the inevitable...

Grant Womack was in love with the picture perfect character she portrayed: the easy-going, witty, free-spirited persona she'd carefully cultivated. He didn't know the *real* Olivia, the one she fought to keep hidden. Because truthfully if he did, he probably wouldn't like her very much.

Olivia stared at the latest issue of Adversity Magazine, the picture she'd submitted of Grant fleeing the theater as it collapsed behind him on the cover. The editor had indicated it was her best work yet and had rewarded her with another sizeable check.

Funny how that accomplishment didn't seem to mean a whole hell of a lot without the man on the cover to share it with...

The sound of her phone ringing startled her,

transporting her back to the here and now. Rising from her gray velvet loveseat, she tossed the magazine on the coffee table and then reached into her purse for her cell phone: KENDALL.

"Hello?"

"Happy birthday!" Kendall squealed.

"Well, not sure I'm 'happy' about turning twenty-eight, but thanks!"

"You okay?" Kendall prodded.

"What? Oh, yeah—I'm fine. I guess I just suddenly realized how close to thirty I'm gettin'."

"It's just a number, ya know", she kindly reminded her.

"Yeah, I guess so. So, anything excitin' happen on the island for New Year's Eve?"

"Nope—just the usual fireworks gathering on the beach... I, ah... ran into Ty."

"Yeah, he mentioned he'd seen you."

"He did?" Kendall asked hopefully. "I mean—yeah, we talked. He was pretty torn-up about not being able to visit for your birthday this year", she amended. No way did her best friend need to know about *everything* that'd happened New Year's Eve!

At least not yet.

"I know. I forget sometimes that not everyone has the flexibility with their careers like I do."

"It's definitely a perk. Running the pharmacy doesn't allow me to take off very often either."

Just then, Olivia's doorbell rang, indicating there was someone just outside the wrought iron gate that led to her small guesthouse. "Hey, listen, someone's at the gate. Ty told me he mailed a package—I bet it's here! Call you back later?"

"Of course", Kendall agreed.

After tossing her cell phone onto the loveseat cushion, she bolted toward the door. Barefoot, she wrapped her arms around herself for warmth and quickly tiptoed to the wrought iron gate. The mailman was long gone, but he'd left her package on the ground on the other side. Once she had it in her grasp, she pranced inside and gave it a gentle shake.

"I wonder what it is?" she mumbled softly. After locating a pair of scissors, she sliced through the tape and unfolded the cardboard flaps, revealing the contents inside: an album.

She expected that Ty had replaced her worn, leather portfolio. But that's not what she saw when she opened to the first page...

Instead, she saw Grant... Turning the page, she relived her time with him back on Butler Island. She hadn't taken all of the pictures; some were probably captured by various friends at various gatherings: poker night, Halloween, Winterfest...

Tears erupted from her eyes as she thumbed through the album. Ty hated the idea of her and Grant—*why had he sent this?* And more importantly, *what'd possessed him to fabricate it in the first place?*

On the very last page was one of her favorite memories of them: the picture captured by her time-lapse feature when Grant had chased her on the beach. Every time she saw it, it made her smile, and this time was no different. Below the picture was a yellow Post-it note that read:

> *Olivia,*
> *Hoping your day will be filled with*
> *unforgettable memories.*
> *All my love,*
> *Grant*

Collapsing onto the loveseat, she clutched the album tightly against her chest and surrendered to the overwhelming wave of despair and regret that'd suddenly washed over her.

Why was she torturing herself? He loved her... and she was in love with him, too.

She loved Grant Womack! There, she admitted it.

Walking away from the man she loved had been much harder than she imagined it would be. Who was she kidding?—she didn't *want* a future of what-if's. Didn't want to deprive herself of his love any longer.

What *did* she want?

Well, that was easy: Grant Womack—no matter if it was six months or sixty years. She just wanted *him*—for as long as he would have her.

Releasing the album from her tight clutch, she glanced at the handwritten note again, savoring each word. It wasn't until she'd re-read it that she noticed a tiny arrow at the bottom, encouraging her to peel the sticky paper away from the page and look on the other side.

Flipping the small yellow paper over, she read the most exciting three words...

Open the gate

A rush of euphoria coursed through her veins. With the album still in her grasp, she hurried toward the door, raced down the porch steps and then ran toward the man that was standing on the other side of the wrought iron gate...

Grant.

* * * * *

It'd taken all of his strength to remain hidden after he pressed the buzzer on her gate. He'd heard it swing open and had been so tempted to reveal his presence. But it wasn't time—not yet.

She was expecting a package from Ty and once she opened it, needed time to digest the contents of the album. And then, she had to digest that the package hadn't come from Ty at all—it'd come from him.

He admitted that normally he was a confident man—but not now. Hell, for all he knew, she'd rip the pages from the binding and toss it in the trash.

After several minutes had elapsed, he ambled toward the gate and waited nervously for the front door to open. He still wasn't sure how he'd be greeted—or if she'd even bother for that matter.

With each passing minute, his anxiety grew; every tick of his watch, his morale weakened. And then, it happened...

The door flew open and the most beautiful woman he'd ever known ran toward him. Her honey-blonde hair had been haphazardly piled on the top of her head, held in place by a pencil; the long sleeve, heather-gray nightshirt hugged her hourglass curves and the hem fell mid-thigh, revealing an incredible pair of legs. But that wasn't the best part. The expression on her face almost rendered him speechless: a beautiful smile and a look in her eyes that revealed more than any words she could've spoken.

She was running toward her future...

Gnawing on her bottom lip, she halted in front

of the gate and stared at a grinning Grant.

"Surprise", he said as he opened his arms.

"I can't believe you're here! I... I thought Chief Handler revoked all vacation time this week?" she asked confusedly.

"All, but one."

"And it *was* Ty's. But he said one of the guys at the department had a family emergency. They needed time off so—"

"—So he gave up his scheduled vacation time... for me", he clarified.

"You?" she asked, bewildered. "Is something wrong?"

"Yeah", he said as he gestured toward the gate between them. "Mind if I come in?"

"I'm sorry, yes, of course you can." Olivia unlocked the gate and opened it. She'd been so surprised to see him, she'd completely forgotten her manners—and not to mention—*her pants!*

Pivoting, she turned toward her front door and tugged on the hem of her gray nightshirt, suddenly aware of how exposed she actually was. Once inside, she gestured for Grant to sit on the loveseat, and then joined him.

"So what's wrong?" she asked impatiently. "It's not your parents, is it?"

"No, although I did visit them on the way here—"

"Grant, that's great! I'm so happy you realized the grudge you've carried with you all these years was trivial. You have two parents who wanna be a part of your life!—do you know what I'd give to have that?"

Grant smiled. "I know. And if not for you, I

honestly don't know if I would've taken that first step."

Uncomfortable with his praise, she tucked her feet underneath her and tugged at the hem of her shirt again. "So if your parents are fine, what's the emergency?"

"It's personal", he uttered softly.

"Oh... I'm sorry. I—"

"—You see", he interrupted, "a very beautiful photographer left town; left me with a hole in my heart... I was hoping you could mend it."

Olivia lowered her head. "Grant, I—"

"No, listen to me", he demanded as he cupped the back of her neck. "I love you. You're a part of me now—you can't just take-off and leave."

"There's so much you don't know about me, Grant. I'm—"

"I know more than you think. You're a smart-ass with a big heart and an infectious laugh; you're talented, you're beautiful, and you're the bravest person I've ever known."

Olivia met his gaze and shook her head. "I'm not brave—I'm a coward. I'm afraid, Grant. I'm so afraid to allow anyone to get too close. And when I feel like someone's broken through the barrier, I push them away. I've never completely lowered my guard before—until you. The more I pushed, the harder you pushed back... I let you get too close, and now... now I'm terrified", she confessed.

"Of what?" he prodded as his thumb brushed her cheek.

Olivia closed her eyes as a tear escaped. She needed to be honest with not only Grant, but herself. And somehow, saying the words with her eyes closed seemed safer. "Terrified that I've found the love of my life—scared that it's only a matter of time before I lose him."

"What?" He questioned optimistically.

Olivia opened her eyes and gnawed on her bottom lip. "I... *I love you."*

The words had barely left her lips before his mouth came over hers. It was fiery and ravenous at first, and then their tongues waltzed to a slow, soothing melody.

A sensual oral promenade.

Breaking the kiss, Grant leaned his forehead against Olivia's and gazed into her vibrant emerald eyes. "Marry me", he blurted.

"What?" she asked in disbelief.

"Livvy, you fill a void in my life I never knew existed. Now that I know, I can't live without you. You're a vital part of me now—I need you like my lungs need air. Please, Livvy, please say yes..."

Those next few seconds were the longest of his entire life. Once the initial shock faded from her angelic face, he knew.

The corners of her mouth turned upward and a radiant glow beamed from her eyes, beckoning him—calling him home.

Olivia nodded and then threw her arms around him.

"I promise I'll make you happy, Livvy; we'll spend a lifetime filling albums with good memories."

And that's when she knew: Although her road to "happily ever after" hadn't been paved, she still managed to find her picture perfect fairytale ending.

Stay tuned for

Nikki Rittenberry's

next Butler Island novel

Coming Fall 2012